# A Rogue's Redemption

*Rogue Series: Book One*

by

## DOMINA ALEXANDRA

**2022**

## Also by Domina Alexandra

*I Belong With Her*

*Love Undercover*

*Endless as the Stars*

*A Night Claimed (Claimed Series book 1)*

*Omega Rising (Claimed Series book 2)*

*An Omega's Grief (Claimed Series book 3)*

I'd like to give a big thanks to my editor Julie Wagner and the entire Triplicity Publishing team for helping make this story come alive.

# Chapter One

*Danni*

I paced frantically in circles, my jagged claws scratching against the metal floor of the cage. There were two-inch-thick bars between me and freedom, a reminder that I wasn't in charge of my life. Being caged seemed to be the only thing I knew. I snarled from deprivation and torment. If I didn't get out of this cage soon, I knew my wolf would take control and I'd do something reckless. I couldn't afford to be reckless. I'd only end up with a new scar to collect on my back.

There was no lighting in the room I'd been kept in, but my wolf's eyes had adjusted. Several mundane wolves howled in anguish, displeased with being caged like me. They were all lined up against the wall, whining to be free and eat. Having been treated like a wild animal for so long, I had begun to believe I was just another wolf in here and nothing more. My wolf wanted to break free and kill something. The cage was barely large enough to fit my long frame. I weighed under 100 pounds, which was considered a bit small for the average werewolf. I had not eaten a meal in two days. My owner liked to starve me. His way of guaranteeing I won every fight.

My ears rose high as footsteps approached. I could tell by scent alone it wasn't my owner. The door swung open; a man with a beard long enough to braid came inside, bringing in a wolf that whined as he dragged it into the room. I knew his name to be Johnson. Someone I'd never wanted to belong to. He was far worse with punishment than my owner. He also ran this establishment.

"Pete, come and open this damn cage for me. My wolf here's pissing me off." Johnson slammed the side of the wolf's face down against the concrete to control it. "Don't make me put you down," he hissed in annoyance. Johnson looked into the wolf's eyes until it whimpered in submission.

"Damn it, Pete," Johnson called out, looking over his shoulder toward the door.

Pete ran into the room, buckling his pants with an overconfident grin on his face. He looked young and naïve, barely old enough to drink, though I could sense he was a couple of decades older. That was one of the things I could always sense from other werewolves. Their true strength and age.

"Dang. I was enjoying a little—"

"I don't give a damn what your dick was in. Open this damn cage. That's your fucking job so make it happen."

"Sorry, Johnson." Pete lost his smile. He moved quickly around Johnson, going to the cage left of me and unlocking it.

I watched as Johnson lifted the wolf and forced it into the cage. When the wolf was inside, Johnson slammed the cage door shut and grunted.

"Fucking animal."

For no other reason than me not liking Johnson, I snarled as he hovered over the wolf he had just locked away. Johnson's eyes shifted my way and narrowed with a warning.

"What are you going to do about it?" he challenged.

In response, my wolf took control for a moment and slammed into the cage, making it shake.

Johnson straightened his posture, surprised by my reaction. To him, I was another mundane wolf. My werewolf scent was hidden by the magic my owner possessed. Johnson was smart enough to know that a normal wolf wouldn't react the way I had. Suspicion crept in his eyes as he studied me, leaving an uneasy sensation swirling in my empty belly.

It was too late to hold back now. My wolf was awake and in need of a fresh kill. I growled; teeth exposed in a threatening manner.

"I'll—" Johnson was about to reach for my cage lock when the one man I loathed to see stepped into the room.

His green eyes fixed on me briefly before shifting to Johnson with a polite smile.

"Is there a problem?" he asked Johnson, who looked ready to kill something himself.

Johnson huffed out, "You better get that wolf of yours under control, Hansel!" He didn't bother saying anything else, storming past Hansel and Pete and back toward where everyone was waiting.

Hansel gave Pete a tight stare, his way of telling him to leave.

With an awkward grin, Pete nodded his head once and left, shutting the door behind him.

The desire to pace was strong but I held myself in place like a statue. My wolf and I had been struggling with control for a long time but at this moment, I'd taken it back. The amount of conditioned fear instilled in me from Hansel's countless beatings in the first few years of my life under his control seemed to overpower any desire to kill him and run free.

"Are you trying to get us caught? It won't be just my ass on the line." Hansel's lips pursed to one side, taking me in. His tone was malicious and suggestive of punishment. He knelt to my cage, studying me harshly.

I lowered my head immediately. I was supposed to act like every other wolf in this room and I had failed. Pretending to be a mundane wolf wasn't as easy as it seemed. The fact that I drew attention to myself was all the proof he needed to know I'd done something.

"You do know, once we are home, I will have to punish you?" Hansel had a way of talking to me as if expecting me to agree and welcome the idea. Since I couldn't use words, Hansel figured I'd agreed and nodded.

He stood up, holding chains in his hand as he unlocked the cage door. My eyes darted to the lock, knowing I'd be free enough to stretch my body. The downside, it was my turn.

"You be a good girl," he ordered. Rough fingers brushed over my head in a possessive gesture rather than comforting touch.

When the cage door opened, I stepped out far enough to allow Hansel to attach the chained leash to my collar. He guided me to the door and right before he opened it, I heard him mutter, "Don't fuck this up for me."

*

Loud cheers came from the main area where everyone would be waiting to see the fight. The double doors opened as the smell of blood perfumed my nose. There was also a foul smell I recognized all too well. Death.

We were in a basketball gym with over 50 people standing at the center of the court, chatting away, and placing their bets. I was always nervous around large crowds. All eyes began to fall on me, assessing my worth. I snarled in warning. I walked, cautious of the slippery tile, claws scratching against the surface.

Hansel held me tightly by the chain around my neck. Eager people stepped out of our way, sensing me as a threat. My eyes landed on the thick plastic cage where I'd be fighting, no more than the length of two parking spaces. I'd fought in worse conditions with limited space.

"Welcome, everyone, to the fight that's kept you here all day." It was Johnson speaking as an announcer. I watched him approach from the other end of the cage, silencing everyone. All eyes were focused on him, eager like predators lusting to see bloodshed. Judging by everyone's scent, most of them were werewolves. When Johnson finally spoke again, he looked toward Hansel with a furtive grin before glancing down at me. He winked at me, and I lowered my eyes realizing he knew the truth, that I was a werewolf.

"I have a special treat for everyone, so you might want to raise your bets or even change them," Johnson continued.

Hansel blew out a harsh breath, drawing the same conclusion I had. This was my fault. If I had not reacted to how he mistreated the wolves, my secret would still be just that. A secret. "Fix your eyes on Hansel's mean bitch of a wolf. Fifteen straight kills in a roll."

Walking up to me, Johnson pointed his index finger in my direction. Instinctively, my wolf moved quickly, snapping my canines but only collecting air. Hansel yanked my leash rough enough to make me stumble back and I whined from the harsh pain, the chain tightening around my neck. To rile me further, Hansel lifted the leash upward forcing me to stand tall on the forefront of my legs. He cut off my air supply until my growl went away before allowing me to breathe properly.

The look exchanged between Hansel and Johnson was expressionless, but I was smart enough to know that Johnson was not happy with what I'd done. Two for two in making both angry.

The crowd looked anxious, waiting on Johnson to determine my fate right on the spot. There was a rule on attacking the host and I'd done just that, even if I hadn't drawn blood.

"As I was saying—this will be an unforgettable fight." Johnson lifted his hand, signaling someone to approach.

From the other end of the room, I could see the crowd opening. I could hear uncontrolled snarls coming my way and knew this wouldn't be a fight like all the others I'd faced. Two wolves appeared as if they'd been starving several days longer than me. They were northwestern wolves, the biggest of the mundane breed. Both were closer to 200 pounds. I was barely at 100. I looked up at Hansel, begging him to pull me out of this fight, but knew it was far too late. There would be no getting out of this.

Johnson chuckled. "Even your wolf knows she won't win," he muttered under his breath, low enough for only Hansel and me to hear. "It's almost like she knows I'm punishing her."

That comment was all Hansel needed. Somehow, by my brief encounter with Johnson he'd figured out I was a werewolf and this moment confirmed it. Hansel's smile was tight and nervous as he tilted his head in a nod. There was no choice but for me to fight or I would be outed and killed right on the spot. Fighting was my only chance of surviving.

Hansel pursed his lips and smiled to the crowd. "My wolf can handle anything you throw at it."

"Even both of them at the same time?" Johnson asked, doubtful.

Hansel's wolf hummed through his chest.

"Even both," he snarled. He spoke with confidence, but I knew he was nervous. I was his source of income and if I died, he'd lose a lot of money.

Johnson nodded and grinned. "Good!"

The man holding both northwestern wolves chuckled. "That little wolf is about to become a snack for my two full grown wolves. I raised them myself."

The crowd went wild with enthusiasm, realizing what was about to occur. My reputation had been well known in the fighting pit, but I'd never faced off against these kinds of wolves. Let alone two.

My heart paced rapidly, wishing I had a way out of this.

Johnson walked over to the man that firmly held his two wolves and directed him toward a front opening hatch that slid upward. The wolves ran inside of the cage, circling.

Quickly, Hansel bent down to me and whispered, "You fucked yourself and potentially me. I have a lot of money riding on you. If you die, I'll go back, find your dead-beat father, and kill him."

I looked into his eyes and knew he was telling the truth. Hansel never bluffed. This time when I stared back at the cage my wolf was fully in control, staring down the threat I needed to face. I would win and kill anything thrown at me because it was the one thing I knew how to do well. Kill.

"Good luck, whoever you are!" Johnson knelt a few feet away as he opened the hatch for me to go through. He smiled and stood, exchanging a brief glance with Hansel before stepping away.

Hansel knelt and began to remove the chain from around my neck and whispered, "Don't forget what I said."

I stepped inside the cage and heard the hatch shut behind me, knowing this was it.

# Chapter Two

*Karissa*

The last thing I needed was to be patronized and unvalued. I'd been a part of this pack all my life and in the last 20 years my uncle had been running it as Alpha. Before that, my mother had been Alpha for the first 78 years of my life. Now at the age of 98, I'd finally reached the status of being a seasoned werewolf, even if I looked in my mid-20's and would for the next few centuries. Thinking about my mother now made me feel sad about how much I'd lost.

I loved our city. Sacramento was the better end of Northern California, with lots of trees and land to run freely through. Being a sentinel wolf had always been a male's position until I came into the picture. I had the ability to detect when a rogue werewolf was trespassing or any wolf outside of my pack. Each wolf had an inherent role to play. My mother understood that more than anyone when she first accepted her place as Alpha. The first female Alpha in the United States, paving the way for a few other female Alphas to accept their status. My parents had accepted what I was and loved me for it, a Sentinel wolf who watched over our territory, investigated, and even eliminated threats who crossed our land and caused harm to my pack or the humans who lived here. I held much responsibility and accepted it without complaint.

But for the last 20 years since my uncle had taken the role of Alpha, he had done everything he could to eliminate my role as Sentinel. Eventually he gave up and just pretended I was off being a submissive wolf until someone told him of something new I'd done.

"What did you do now?" Jenkins walked into the waiting room of my uncle's office that was used for pack business. Jenkins had been one of the few werewolves my uncle brought along during his takeover as Alpha and the only one I had a good relationship with. As for the members of my pack I had grown up with, they adored me but feared my uncle and that meant being silent in his presence. I couldn't be mad at them for not taking my side when my uncle and I had disagreements. I was his blood, but they were even less valued.

I'd been sitting in the chair deep in my thoughts and had not noticed Jenkins sitting next to me until he spoke. I rolled my eyes from his assumption that I'd done something wrong.

"Who knows," I said and leaned into my chair. I gave a brief glance at Jessi, my uncle's receptionist and youngest daughter, and smiled. "He probably found out I was about to go on a patrol when one of his loyal pups ratted me out."

"You are aware, it's their job to tell your uncle everything?" Jenkins said, defending them. He cared about me and the other members that he'd been with for years. I didn't expect him to take my side. The important thing was, he never took anyone's side even when I wished he'd take mine.

I shrugged. "I'm not pissed at them. I get it. But I am who I am, and I won't pretend." I glanced at the white painted walls that held no decorations other than the vase of flowers on Jessi's desk. The place gave off a bored and draining energy. My uncle thought buying a small building and turning it into an office and training center for the pack was a great idea. Each day that went by, this pack felt more like a business and less like family.

Jenkins began to chew on a toothpick, and I snatched it out his mouth. He always made an annoying sound every time he chewed on something, even as a wolf. Though Jenkins looked in his mid- 30's, he was almost 300 years old and very capable of stopping me from pulling a toothpick from his mouth. He grinned as his brown eyes locked on mine. He leaned back into his chair, running his fingers through his short curly hair. I thought of how much our friendship had grown and all he'd taught me in the last 20 years and smiled. He'd come to America not by choice, having grown up as a child in West Africa. He wore his dark skin with pride and never lowered his head for anyone, even when he was a slave.

"Before you ask, I didn't rat you out. I just know as soon as you and your uncle are done arguing, he will call and tell me to follow you. I'm just saving some time getting here early."

I snorted and rolled my eyes.

"My dad's ready for you," Jessi announced, sympathy in her eyes. She was barely 20 and already had her shit figured out. I smiled and leaned over to kiss her cheek before I walked toward my uncle's office.

"We both know how this will end but try to keep your comments to a minimum," Jenkins said, waving me goodbye.

I walked down the narrow hall; my uncle's office was the first door on the right. Being polite, I knocked first before opening it. My uncle didn't believe in the 'open door policy.'

"Come in," he said in a low tone.

When I opened the door, I found my uncle standing over his desk, pouring himself a glass of bourbon. Alcohol did nothing for werewolves except make us appear normal. Christof Lansing was not a man who liked to repeat himself, and he expected me to follow his command. But I'd made him do that more times than I could count for the last 20 years, and I partially took pleasure in pissing him off. He was a few inches past six feet with a lean build. He was over 500 years old with the features of a man in his 40's.

He sat down and I knew it would take him a few seconds more to scrutinize me. His grey eyes locked onto mine and I averted my head, trying not to anger him quickly by staring him down. To a dominant werewolf, lingering eye contact was a form of challenging another to a fight for range or pure defiance.

"Alpha," I greeted.

My uncle grunted and took a sip of his bourbon. "I know you don't agree with everything I have done for this pack..." he paused, his eyes continuing to hover, expecting me to blurt out something sarcastic. When he realized I wasn't going to say anything, he continued.

"Our pack has flourished since I took my place as Alpha. Our finances have tripled. We have been able to build safer dens for our pack. So, why must you continuously wander off and do work that you aren't meant to do?"

I sucked in a breath, mentally cursing him. He'd already started off on a negative high note. "My mother was an amazing and well-respected Alpha, so please stop implying you came and saved this pack." I tried my best not to sound too hostile, but he did an excellent job at pushing my buttons. "As for you tripling our finances, this is true. But I think if you spent more time with the pack and less time treating us all like a business, you'd get a lot more out of being an Alpha."

I knew my words hit home by how hard my uncle's glass slammed against the wooden surface of the desk.

Now that he was upset, I figured there was no point in holding back my words.

"I am sure you don't want to open up the topic of where my place is supposed to be since it would only get you worked up. This pack has been safe, but I wouldn't say safer. Werewolves outside of this pack don't trust or respect you."

"That's enough," he snarked.

I ignored him, falling into one of my rants, arms crossed in defiance.

"Furthermore," I continued, "they find it easier to sneak in and out of our borders because you continuously undermine my role as pack Sentinel. I am the only one who can sense when our pack has a new werewolf in our territory." At this point my hand was swaying all over the place and I was ready to call him every name in the book. I could hear my uncle in the background, telling me to silence but I continued to ignore him. I had a temper, and once it was let out it was hard to put back in the cage. "Let's not forget the meeting the rogue wolves wanted to set up with you, and you ignored them as if they were shit you just polluted in the goddamn toilet. You have more enemies than you care to acknowledge and one day—"

"I've said enough," my uncle snarled, standing up this time with gold eyes and fist tightly bawled.

I briefly stared him down, but only for a few seconds. I knew I'd crossed the line but honestly, I didn't care. This pack was my mothers, and he was ruining the good parts of it.

"I have put up with your continuous disrespect for far too long," he snarled.

"Now you see how I feel," I muttered loudly enough for him to hear.

My uncle moved around his desk so quickly that he was pinning me against the wall before I had time to detect his approach, fingers tight around my neck.

I did not hesitate or flinch. As a Sentinel, the one advantage I had against an Alpha was the desire to take care of pack and territory first before an Alpha's needs. As a Sentinel wolf, I lacked the fear of an Alpha like all the other werewolves, second to another Alpha and a lone wolf.

"You call me?" Jenkins walked into the office, standing near the door playing my hero. Jenkins shot me a wink as my uncle's back was turned from him. We both knew my uncle hadn't called him.

My uncle took a step back and allowed me room to breathe. After a long pause and me waiting for him to say something else, my uncle walked back to his desk.

"I am only obligated to keep you in this pack for another 30 years unless you break pack law."

Luckily for me, pack law was written by the werewolf council and not him. And the pack law stated that if a new Alpha took over another territory, he or she could not force a long-standing member of that pack for the first 50 years unless that member posed as a risk to the pack. I didn't respect my uncle as my Alpha, but I respected the role of an Alpha and its members. And as much as my uncle hated it, my role as Sentinel was acknowledged by the council and I'd only been doing my job as Sentinel long before he'd taken over, despite his heavy protest. There was a reason I'd decided to stay in this pack, and it was not because I was afraid to find a new one. There were a lot of progressive Alphas out there more than willing to accept me into their pack, just for being a Sentinel. This was my mother's pack, and it deserved a better Alpha. And I'd stay until I found the right Alpha. That was another crucial factor my uncle hated. If I could prove to the council that my uncle was unfit as Alpha, I could get him demoted because at the end of the night, my first duty was to the pack and their safety. He had yet to do anything that I could bring to the council, but I knew it was only matter of time.

I bit my tongue just as I was about to say something that might get my uncle to do more than choke me, but I was ready to leave and kept my snide comments to myself.

"If there isn't anything else. I'd like to continue with my job," I said instead.

My uncle looked to Jenkins, who nodded.

"On it, boss!" Jenkins smiled and looked to me.

I didn't bother saying anything else to my uncle and walked out. When I made it to the front of the office, I waved and smiled with relief that I could finally continue with my duty to the pack.

\*

"How do you know they are here without anything to track them with?" Jenkins asked, always fascinated by how being a Sentinel worked. Not every pack had a Sentinel. On average packs typically had only submissive, dominant betas, two trackers and an Alpha. For every 10 packs there was one Sentinel. Most Alphas were thankful, unlike my uncle. I had learned that usually an Alpha who was unhappy in having a Sentinel wolf knew they couldn't be malicious to their members without being brought to justice.

I shrugged. "I just do," I said. "It's like the feeling you get when you need to shift on a full moon, but instead my heart flutters with anxiety and I just know."

I stepped out of the car noticing a few people headed to the main entrance of the building. It was midday and the sun would be down in a few hours. I didn't want anyone recognizing me so I hoped masking myself with shades and a hoodie would do the trick. We were in the parking lot of a youth center that had closed months ago. It was on the edge of our city of Sacramento and close enough for uninvited werewolves to slip in and out of my territory. I'd known the moment non-pack werewolves entered my territory and where they were, usually within seconds.

I'd been casing the place for the last two days, getting a sense of what they were doing here before I decided to barge inside like an undercover officer.

"So, what are they up to?" Jenkins asked, closing the car door.

"They've turned the place into an illegal fighting ring for mundane wolves."

Jenkins whistled. "Damn!"

I watched as a small group of men headed for the door, holding out 100 dollars in each of their hands. I listened closely, using my werewolf hypersensitive hearing as they whispered, "Bite me hard."

The person working the door nodded and took their money. We were about 50 feet away when I bumped my arm into Jenkins.

"Pull out a 100," I said.

Jenkins narrowed his eyes and frowned, knowing he had no choice. We walked up to the door where the man stood. He stared at both of us as Jenkins held out a 100.

Before Jenkins tried to repeat the words we had overheard the last guys say, I said, "My boyfriend's a bad wolf!" I looked up and winked at Jenkins who only smiled, taking my words literally. Not the boyfriend part but being called a bad wolf. He knew he wasn't my type.

The guy at the door nodded and took the money from Jenkins hand.

"Bet hard. The final match is going to be a big one."

Jenkins nodded. "Will do!"

We walked inside where there was a large opening before the double doors that led to the inside of a basketball gym. I could hear people shouting out their bets as the smell of death floated in the air.

The moment we entered the gym, we walked toward where the crowd of people stood, surrounding a huge cage. There was even a large projector up, giving a better view to the crowd pushed to the back.

"Fuck! How the hell is that small ass wolf going to survive two Northwestern wolves?" a man blurted out to his friend, chuckling.

The man beside him shrugged. "All I know is the other wolf is known to be possessed. It might look harmless, but I wouldn't fuck with it."

I frowned and looked toward the projector. There were two wolves inside the cage, pacing as if eager to kill something. Instinct tugged at my chest, and I suddenly had the urge to get closer to the cage. Someone important was there and I needed to find them.

I tapped Jenkin's shoulder. "Come on! I have a feeling this won't be ending well."

Jenkins frowned and shook his head. "Never is with you!"

I glanced up at the projector just as the smaller wolf was forced inside. Its black fur was thick and long, with a narrow frame. Against two northwestern wolves, it would be almost impossible to beat.

There was a VIP line barricaded by a rope when we approached. A man with thick bushy brows frowned at the sight of us approaching and took a step, blocking our access. He was brawny and perfect for security.

"This is only for high bet dealers and sponsors."

"You can make an exception, can't you?" I smiled widely, hoping to bring a little charm to this undercover work.

The man didn't react in my favor and looked more annoyed.

"No!" He pointed to where others stood and watched from the projector screen. "That's where you two belong."

I frowned and shifted toward the projector.

"But that's not good enough," I complained.

"Do you want me to remove you?" the guy asked in a threatening tone.

Jenkin's smiled and tugged me away. "She can be a little pushy." He guided me away from the man. "What's the big deal?" he asked when we were at a safe distance to talk.

I sighed. I felt a need to be right next to the cage, and the longer it took the more anxiety I felt. Something was pulling me there and my wolf would claw her way out to get to it. I watched in agony as the fight began, people cheering and calling out bets. The two wolves lunged for an attack as the smaller wolf rushed past both and darted side to side from every attack. The black wolf was fast. My heart raced and my lungs tightened as one of the northwestern wolves twisted quickly and raked its claws across the smaller black wolf's face. Blood was drawn and the crowd cheered, most of them werewolves.

I'd felt the presence of unknown werewolves in our territory but not this many well established ones so soon. It made sense to have humans here. They were probably paid weeks ago to come and set this place up for them.

Most of these wolves were all new to me, apart from a few I'd chased out of our territory on a few occasions. My eyes couldn't leave the screen as the smaller wolf fought for its life, dodging most of the other two wolves' blows. I watched every motion the smaller wolf made, willing the black wolf to fight harder.

One of the northwestern wolves' fangs pierced the black wolf's back leg. My eyes flared gold. I began to growl, every breath I took heavy and loud. I could feel my claws digging into the palms of my hand. The black wolf tried to pull free, but the other wolf was too strong. The second northwestern wolf came fast smashing its body against the black wolf and then lunged for its neck. The black wolf snarled and moved as if possessed, yanked its leg free somehow and tore into one of the northwestern wolves' bellies. Blood spilled instantly.

Everyone stood on edge as I felt heat flood into my body. My wolf was awake and ready to come out.

Hands touched me and I snarled, twisting my head, ready for a kill. It was Jenkins. I lowered my hand, realizing I was inches from hitting him. He took a step back, shocked by my reaction.

"What the fuck?" he hissed.

"I'm done watching this. I need to get to that cage. Now!" I snarled so loudly that several werewolves turned to face me instead of watching the fight.

I twisted quickly, heading back to the VIP section. The werewolf bouncer noticed me coming and tried to stand in my way. I reached for the arm he held out and grabbed his thumb, twisting it upwards and forcing him to position his arm in an awkward outward angle. I slammed my other hand into the center of his chest. His sternum bone snapped, and I kicked him hard in the balls, making my way toward the cage. I took off the sunglasses and lowered my hoodie from my head.

Werewolves moved out my way quickly, a path to the cage opening. My eyes darted to a man with a long beard who I easily recognized. I watched him speak to someone, the sound of everyone else around distorting his words.

Two werewolves stepped into my line of view and Jenkins came at that perfect moment, extending his arms and slamming both to the ground in a pro wrestler move.

In the background, I heard my name shouted.

"It's Karissa! The pack Sentinel."

And just like that, everyone began running. I shifted my glance, attempting to search for the long-bearded man but he was gone.

"I got these two," Jenkins assured me.

I nodded and headed to the cage. The fight between the wolves was still active; the black wolf had managed to kill one, even with an injury of its own. The black wolf limped as the last Northwestern wolf leaped for it. The black wolf leaped at the same time, catching the other wolf by its throat and dropping on top of it. I watched as it ripped the Northwestern's neck open, and my jaw dropped.

Despite such odds, the black wolf had killed two northwestern wolves. The black wolf snarled repeatedly and paced as if it needed to find something new to kill.

My heart drummed in my chest at the sight. The cage floor was covered in blood but all I had the instinct to do was crawl inside. I felt like I was right where I was supposed to be, and I didn't know what that meant. I moved to open the hatch and allow it a chance to get out.

"What are you doing?" Jenkins asked. "That thing is too wild to listen to you."

When the wolf's eyes finally found mine, I shook my head, realizing the truth. It was like I could see inside the wolf's heart and intentions.

"She won't hurt me."

I took several steps back, signaling for Jenkins to do the same. I never took my eyes off the black wolf. She was beautiful and fierce, even covered in blood.

The wolf studied me and then Jenkins for a long time. She didn't move, cautious of our presence.

Jenkins pointed his finger toward the wolf. She snarled; teeth exposed.

"I don't think this—"

"Don't point at her! She doesn't like that," I chastised.

"How the hell do you know?" he asked quietly.

I had no idea.

"Hey," I called out. "It's just you and me. Ignore the idiot who hasn't figured you out yet," I said, hoping she would understand.

When the wolf's eyes shifted back to me, I knew my instincts were right. My heart skipped a beat. I nodded toward the two dead wolves.

"Nice work you did."

The wolf huffed as if speaking to me.

I smiled.

"That's not a mundane wolf, is it?" Jenkins finally realized.

I snorted. "He can be a little slow sometimes," I told the black wolf. Jenkins chuckled but said nothing. "Mind shifting back for me?"

The wolf took a step back as if my words frightened her.

I lifted both hands high. "I promise. I am no threat to you."

As if I'd said everything wrong, the wolf ran to the far end of the cage and began looking around as though searching for someone. I glanced around, half expecting someone to appear. I hadn't noticed how empty and quiet it was, too entranced by her.

"Jenkins. Go check to see if there's anyone lingering."

"Got it," he nodded and ran off.

I smiled at the wolf again. "Now it's just you and me!" I walked toward the cage slowly, not wanting to make any sudden movements that would send her into a panic. "Mind if I come in?"

If I knew anything, this werewolf had been abused. She stayed motionless, giving me space to crawl in. I knew this might be awhile.

# Chapter Three

*Danni*

I was back in control and now faced with a woman who seemed strange to want to be caged inside with me. She was free and could leave with no questions asked but instead she lingered. I was a wild and monstrous animal with no control over my actions. What was she trying to do by staying?

The fight with the two northwestern wolves had been a blur. Anytime my wolf took over I was only left with aches and small picture clips in my mind of what had occurred.

The woman couldn't stand without hitting her head against the top of the cage ceiling, so she decided to crouch instead. Despite my initial hesitation to run from her, some foreign part of me told me to trust her. Her gray eyes squinted, the curve of her lips forming a smile. I lifted my snout high enough to firmly catch her scent and hesitated to move. She carried a similar smell to me. She was a werewolf too.

"My name's Karissa. By your curiosity, I'm sure you have figured out that I'm a werewolf." Her voice was soft and melodic like someone who took pleasure in soothing others. She had long brunette hair and gray eyes. There was no doubting that she was a fighter from her toned arms and slender build, reminding me of all the women in TV shows that played the healer and protector. I sensed that her wolf was extraordinarily strong too.

"I hear this isn't your first fight," she went on, managing to come closer to me without getting near the dead wolves. "It would be a whole lot easier if I could speak to you."

Instinctively, I looked back toward the front of the gym as someone walked through the doors. It was the woman's friend. I searched for Hansel at every corner, but I couldn't see or smell him.

The woman tilted her head to me before gazing around.

"Are you looking for someone?" she asked.

My eyes darted back to her as I stood on all fours, motionless and not sure what to do. Hansel had left me. He'd never done that before.

"There's no one around except the two guys I locked in the back of our car, still unconscious. Neither has your scent on them so I know they're not who you keep searching for." Karissa's friend explained.

He came up to the cage wearing a worried expression. "What the hell are you doing inside?" he asked the woman who wasn't afraid of me.

I wondered if he owned her by his tone but immediately shook that thought away. No! Karissa seemed like she was in charge. Hansel had told me women werewolves were not given leadership roles. He also said he would never leave me and here I was now.

"Please!" the woman spoke softly to me. Her thin lips formed into a smile when I acknowledged her with eye contact. "I can't leave you here and I'm sure you must be tired. Tired of a lot of things. I want to be your ally. Friend. If you trust even an ounce of what I'm saying, shift and talk to me." She spoke quickly as if she didn't have much time left to reason with me, which made me look back toward the exit.

I hadn't changed from my wolf in three years and at this point I didn't know if it was possible to shift back. I lowered my head in defeat, wishing for the first time in those three years that I could shift back for her.

"I think she doesn't know how to," I heard the man say.

I looked up to him straight away, hoping she could see that I was agreeing with his statement.

He pointed his finger at me. "See!"

An alarm rang in my head, my wolf's teeth gritting toward him. My wolf and I were tired of fingers pointing at us. Since being a werewolf, I had known the gesture to mean two things: to insult or blame me for something right before a beating.

"Put your hand down, Jenkins," Karissa hissed, never taking her eyes off me.

The man she called Jenkins dropped his hand right away.

"My bad," he said, looking my way.

My teeth were still exposed but the humming in my chest lessened.

I heard more people coming inside and used my nose. More werewolves.

"What the hell is she doing in a cage with a wild rogue?" A man in a black suit snarled as he approached. His brown hair was neatly kempt with his expression creased into a frown. He studied me for a few seconds longer than my comfort level allowed and I knew he was much older than even Hansel. I growled, not trusting that he had kind intentions toward me.

"Alpha," Karissa said, and the older man crossed his arms, giving her his attention. "Upon doing my job, I discovered non-pack werewolves in our territory running an illegal fighting pit with mundane wolves."

"That is no mundane." He pointed toward me.

I snarled loud enough to have all eyes shift my way. If one more person pointed at me, I'd run out of this cage and bite off every finger I saw.

"Drop your hand, please!" Karissa ordered the man.

He hesitated but did so anyway.

"I am aware of her being a werewolf. But there seems to be a problem. She is unable to shift back. If you could please assist with that," she asked in a tone that told me she did not like this man. Perhaps she was owned by him.

I couldn't understand what was going on and who these werewolves were.

The man looked to me with a hidden expression. "Fine! Only because we need to know who she is and who to send her back to." He stepped next to the cage and locked eyes with me as he whispered, "Shift."

I looked at him in confusion. Was that supposed to work? I looked to the woman as if she were going to explain what I was supposed to do to move the process along.

"It didn't work," one of the men said.

"I can see that," the man with authority said in frustration. "Perhaps—"

The woman moved closer to me in the middle of the man speaking.

I took a step back, nervous about what she might do.

"Trust me," she whispered.

And as if she'd compelled me, I relaxed enough to let her reach for me. We were inches apart as our eyes never wavered from one another. Something about her calmed me and assured me that I could trust her. I was in a cage, covered in blood, injured, and I'd let a stranger reach in to touch me. Part of me was perplexed by my wolf's eagerness to allow Karissa to get this close. When her hand brushed the top of my head, my body began to tingle as everything my wolf and I had been holding onto finally decided to temporarily slip away. I felt myself begin to shift. It was not violent or painful like I remembered it to be, but more like stretching my limbs after a long workout.

When it was all over, I curled into a ball with no desire to move as my eyes fell shut, cherishing this moment.

\*

*Karissa*

"What did you do to her?" Jenkins asked in a humorous tone, crouching next to the hatch opening.

I shook my head, unable to speak. The woman lay curled tightly and peacefully, as if she had not slept in months. Ignoring the two dead wolves in the cage I moved around, crawling on hands and knees so I wouldn't startle her restless body.

"Just leave her so we can talk privately," my uncle ordered.

His words held no value as I continued to close the distance between the woman and me. When I made it to her side, I admired her dark complexion, perfect even covered in bruises and blood. A faint scar marked the right side of her face, but that would be healed within the next hour. Her tightly coiled black chin length hair fell over her face; eyes shut from exhaustion. I had an impulse I never thought I'd crave, a need to touch her so profoundly that it sent my wolf into a frenzy. Chills ran down my back and arms and I ignored the fear dancing at the tip of my thoughts. As much as I wondered what this feeling was inside me, I wanted to know what her skin felt like even more.

"Karissa! For once in your fucking life. Listen to me," I heard my uncle holler in the background. He was too proper an Alpha to crawl through and pull me out.

I shut him out of my mind as I focused only on the woman. She'd been the one to draw me to this cage. That need to protect could not be forgotten. My hands shook as I leaned over her naked body, reaching to brush a strand of her hair from her face. When the tips of my fingers brushed her cheek, my wolf shuddered and I inhaled slowly, hot with an unexpected sensation. A tear slipped from my eyes as I watched her for what felt like forever.

The woman jolted, startled from my touch. She slid her back against the edge of the cage, glancing around and noticing my pack.

I smiled weakly. "Hi!" I was unable to find any other words and blushed.

The woman looked into my eyes, trying to remember who I was. When her tense shoulders eased, I mentally sighed, relieved that I wasn't forgotten.

"I didn't mean to scare you," she whispered timidly, voice raspy from lack of use. Her brown eyes softened on mine.

I shook my head. "I'm fine."

She frowned and reached out, using her thumb to wipe away my tear. "You are crying!"

Her arms were long with broad shoulders and a lean build, and I was impressed that she carried so much muscle when her wolf was the size of a newly turned.

"The Alpha will have my head if you don't come out," Jenkins protested, hunched over and sticking his head inside of the cage.

I groaned, briefly acknowledging Jenkins with a nod before looking back to the woman.

"I have to go speak with someone. Will you come out with me?"

The woman looked at every person in the room. By now there were 11 of my pack members inside, either standing guard or just watching us.

"I promise no one will touch you," I told her.

She studied me for some time and considered, continuing to watch everyone. I could see she doubted my words, only observing everyone around. Her eyes narrowed on someone for a few seconds before she sneered. I didn't need to see who she had been staring at. My uncle was easy to detect as the distrusting one.

"If they lunge at me, I will attack. It is my first instinct to kill, and I don't have control," she warned me.

I nodded, wanting to remind her that it was in all our natures to kill, but something told me she was speaking in a different context than the normal day to day werewolves who mostly hunted game. Based on the fight I witnessed, I had no doubt she could hold her own.

"Fair warning to the idiot who tries to touch you. They can all hear you and I'm sure if they're smart, they'll listen." I was speaking to my pack, making sure they got the message. As Sentinel, it was my duty to maintain peace even within the pack and if there were Omegas it would be a combined effort to get that task done with minimum to no bloodshed.

The woman squinted her eyes, staring past me. "I don't want to get you in trouble."

"Let me worry about that."

I moved to the exit and hoped she followed. The last thing the woman needed was me hovering and making her look weak when she was far from it. When I slid out the other end, I stood and turned to find her right behind me. She was a bit wobbly crawling out, legs trembling as if she hadn't walked on them in month. I offered my hand and she hesitated, glancing around as she leaned against the outside of the cage. I glanced down at her left leg, noticing newly healed puncture marks where one of the wolves had bitten her.

She sighed. "I can't stand. My legs are weak. I haven't shifted in a long time."

I nodded and clenched my jaw shut, holding back my words. What kind of person would do this to her?

"I need to speak to the man who keeps calling me, but I won't leave your sight," I said.

The woman nodded and watched me walk to the other end of the gym where my uncle and everyone else stood near the front entrance. I smiled to her one last time before facing my uncle fully.

As soon as I came within reach, my uncle grabbed me tightly by the chin with his index finger and thumb.

"Girl! I am beyond sick of you not falling in line."

Dean, one of our elder wolves who I'd known since I was born, tapped my uncle's shoulder. His gray hair was trimmed short, with pale grey eyes and a round soft face that made him look younger than what he was.

"I think it is wise if you let her go," he advised. Elder wolves were considered the great-grandfathers to all wolves, pack mentors, living at least six centuries. It would be an insult for my uncle not to listen to him.

My uncle twisted his head toward the woman sitting against the cage and frowned. She was looking directly at him, eyes a raw gold. Her expression skewed into a frown as she watched and never blinked, ready to attack if he made one wrong choice. Making a wise decision, my uncle slowly lowered his hand. I could feel his temptation to kill the woman and I was surprised he hadn't acted on the impulse yet. His brows kneaded together, deep in thought.

When I was free of his grip, I twisted to fully get a view of her. The woman was still watchful of my uncle. I stood still, not sure how to react. No one had ever stood up for me to such a degree.

"Why do you continuously defy me?" My uncle hissed.

"It isn't my intention to upset you. But as Sentinel, it is my priority to protect the pack and our territory, even if you hate it," I argued.

"Then get rid of her, as you keep claiming to be a Sentinel. I will deal with you at pack home." My uncle turned to leave, expecting that to be the end of conversation.

Dean gave me a knowing smile, already sensing what I was about to say. For a werewolf over 600 years old, Dean hadn't lost his ability to see between the lines. If anything, he was much clearer than anyone else.

I wasn't ready for what was to come, but I knew who she was the moment I touched her. I couldn't send her away and pretend she meant nothing.

"No! She will come back to the pack, as it is stated by pack law when one is left in need," I said.

My uncle ended his stride and turned to face me with wide eyes. Everyone else stood like statues.

"Only if given permission by an Alpha or you have turned, mated, or become indebted to one that needs solace."

"My wolf has claimed her as mate," I said, loud enough for each of them to hear me.

31

My uncle twisted and glanced at the woman and then back to me. I could see it in his eyes that he wanted to contest the claim. He was too conservative to believe two female werewolves could legitimately mate.

"It is true," Dean said in defense of me.

I nodded my head to him in thanks and smiled.

My uncle narrowed his eyes on the woman and back to me then huffed.

"Fine. She can stay, but do not bring her into our pack home until we know more."

"That is fine. She will come home with me," I said.

My uncle waved me off and turned to leave. This time I didn't stop him as I watched him go, taking most of the pack.

"You want me to go with you?" Jenkins asked.

"No. We both know my uncle will want to interrogate you about everything," I said.

He nodded. "True." He smiled and shook his head in disbelief. "Your mate had to be a wild one just like you. How fitting."

I rolled my eyes and flipped him off.

"Thank you," I said, bowing my head to Dean for standing up for me.

He nodded. "I see that you and this new mate of yours are only at the beginning of something large and special. There will be a lot of dark nights before it is bright. But I hold confidence in you, and in her. She's more important to the future than anyone knows." Dean smiled and walked out.

I watched him leave, taking in his words. When I turned back around, I found the woman watching me. We were alone and I had no idea how to convince her to come with me. What was that saying? *Try. And then try again!* Or something like that.

# Chapter Four

*Danni*

The woman walked nervously back to me. I wondered what had happened to all the confidence Karissa had before she spoke with the man. When his hand touched her, I'd felt provoked and ready to rip his throat out as if he had personally caused me harm. And now I wondered if he was leaving her here as punishment like Hansel had done to me.

I pressed the palm of my hand against the cage, attempting to propel myself up. I hadn't used human legs in so long, it took time remembering how to walk. I stumbled, trying to keep my balance as my knees buckled.

Karissa rushed to my side in time to assist me and I stood straight on both legs. Her eyes hardened but she said nothing. Something was bothering her.

"Did your owner hurt you?" I asked, cautiously. I thought about the man's hand on her again and frowned.

She paused and gave me a confused look.

"Owner?" she repeated.

"Alpha," I said, nodding my head toward the door. "That's the name you used when you called him."

The woman seemed to understand and nodded. "Oh, Alpha isn't his name. Its's like a title. Role or status. I'm not owned. No one should be owned."

I hesitated, not sure what to say. I stared off toward the entrance, instinctively searching for Hansel again. Since entering this world as a werewolf, property was all I knew how to be.

"Hey," Karissa mumbled softly.

I lifted my gaze back toward her and sighed. "If he doesn't own you then why did he touch you like that?" I needed to understand how she was any different from me.

I could tell my question hit home by the way her eyes wavered, deep in thought.

"You didn't hear anything we talked about?" she asked.

I shook my head. "I've been taught never to listen in," I explained.

Karissa nodded and took a step back, gradually giving me more room to hold my own balance. Her eyes thoroughly took me in from top to bottom, and I saw fear flare in her pupils for a moment. Was she afraid of me?

"Do you remember my name?" she asked, snatching me from my thoughts.

I nodded. "Part of it is a little fuzzy, but I remember your name," I stated.

"Lansing is my last name," she added.

I nodded. I hadn't introduced myself in a decade. Part of me wasn't sure if I should tell her, knowing it was only a matter of time before Hansel took me back. But as I gazed into her eyes, I could see it mattered to her and I didn't want to disappoint.

"Danni," I spoke softly.

"Just Danni?" she asked.

I paused and considered. I thought of my past before I became what I was now and frowned. I'd lost so much time as a human that it was hard to give myself a full name.

That meant I belonged somewhere other than with Hansel once. And I couldn't open that door.

Karissa waved her hand.

"Don't worry about it," she said as she glanced around. "Would you like to come home with me?" She squinted her eyes as if she'd said something wrong. "I mean…I don't think it's safe for you to stay here and I'm sure you are hungry."

I was now able to stand firmly on both legs. Taking my first step, I felt like a toddler all over again. Luckily, my muscle memory was slowly kicking in. I took one last glance around, wondering where Hansel could be. I was hungry and I liked being near her.

"Who do you keep looking for?" Karissa asked, glancing around with me.

I looked directly at her, stopping myself from looking around. Hansel told me if we were ever separated to never reveal to anyone who he was. It was not a rule I was going to break now.

"No one," I said, feeling a bit uncomfortable. I also knew Hansel would want me to stay put, but something told me Karissa wouldn't let me stay here without her at my side.

"So?" she asked.

I sighed. "Okay, if you are sure."

"I am!" Karissa took off her sweater and offered it to me. "Probably not a great idea to go out exposed."

I nodded and took it as she helped me put it on.

"My car is close. If we move quickly, no one will see you," Karissa assured me. I thanked her and followed behind closely, knowing wherever I was headed would be a brief stay.

### Karissa

We made it to my house within 30 minutes, pulling into the garage. Once the door was shut, I turned off the car and unbuckled my seatbelt. The entire drive was quiet as I occasionally peaked toward Danni. I hadn't acknowledged the most important part I'd learned tonight. That she was my mate.

When I exited the car, I turned to find her still sitting inside.

"You can come in," I told her.

Danni looked paralyzed, unable to make eye contact. I moved around the car cautiously. I knew she wouldn't hurt me. Even if she was unaware of what we were to each other, her wolf had also claimed me too. I opened the door, kneeling beside her stiff frame.

"Hey." I almost reached for her hand but held back.

I looked down at her lap, where her fingers were curled into a fist. Blood seeped around her fingers, coming from the palm of her hand. I took a breath, reaching in despite my fears, and unraveled her fingers. Her nails had partially shifted into claws, induced from anxiety and confusion. It was evident this was all new to Danni, someone being kind to her without strings attached. Absently, I brushed my hand against her cheek, pulling her eyes to me.

When our eyes locked, Danni took in a slow breath, finally regaining control.

"You are safe and free to come into my home," I said.

A tear slid down her cheek.

"I haven't been in a home since…" her voice trailed off.

"Since when?" I asked, suddenly angered. What kind of life had she been living and for how long?

"I am twenty-four now. So…" she considered and then looked into my eyes. "Since I was 1fifteen."

I held in my tears, trying to be strong for her. My jaw clenched in and out, wanting to shift and find the one responsible.

"You were turned at fifteen?" I asked, baffled. It was rare for a teenage girl to be turned successfully. Most teens who were bitten died from the fever, and the small percentage that successfully turned didn't make it past the first year. Being an adolescent werewolf meant erratic behavior that tended to get them killed.

She nodded. "He—" she stopped herself. "I have been owned since the night I was taken. Turned and made to fight in fighting pits and do other things." She shook her head. "Why am I telling you these things? I don't know you. You don't know me." Danni looked conflicted and unsure of what to say next.

*It was a natural thing to do with a mate, that's why,* I thought. Even if we wanted nothing to do with each other, our wolves would feel differently. You couldn't turn your back on a mate.

"Please. Come inside with me."

She hesitated but eventually moved out of the car.

Once inside, I immediately went to my bedroom to grab fresh clothes for her. I held them out and she took them slowly.

"They might be a little small but should fit well enough. And a towel to shower." She was a few inches taller than me and had a long frame with broad shoulders that would make the shirt tighter around her chest.

I guided her into the bathroom and walked back into my living room, making a quick call to Jenkins the moment the door was shut. I knew whoever had turned Danni had to have been there, and I wanted Jenkins to go and try to find his scent. Danni carried a unique scent that held small traces of lemongrass and magic. Every turned werewolf carried their maker's scent.

By the time I was off the phone with Jenkins, I heard the bathroom door opening. I slid my phone in my back pocket and smiled. I'd been doing that a lot in the past hour, not sure of what other reaction to give her but a smile, as if I were trying to assure her and myself that everything was going to be okay. Truth was, I didn't know what I was doing.

I took in her presence and found myself staring at her nipples that could not be concealed by the tight shirt she wore. I swallowed down my fleshly thoughts, focusing on what mattered right now. Sex with a stranger who had a whole lot of problems and demons to sort through was not the right path to go down, not to mention my own promise to never fall in love. Danni's brown eyes stared back at me intensely, trying to decipher my thoughts. There was this dangerous aura about her that excited my wolf, in a good way.

"Are you sure you want me here?" she asked, looking toward the door.

"What?" I asked, startled by her question. I laughed and shook my head. "Oh, no. I am just in my head. I think a lot. About everything."

She nodded. "Thank you for the clothes. You have been more than kind to me." She smiled politely as if she had been rehearsing that in the bathroom.

The way Danni spoke gave me the impression she was trying to be careful with her words.

"So, how about some food?" I offered, trying to change the topic and take my eyes away from her long enough to breathe properly.

She nodded.

It took 30 minutes for the pizza delivery to arrive. I made sure I ordered every meat ingredient they had. When werewolves were under stress or any other physical or emotional duress, we ate double the amount of food. As soon as I handed Danni the plate, she had devoured her food faster than anyone I'd seen before.

I watched as she ate the entire box. When she was done, she licked her fingers, closing her eyes as if she were embedding this memory into her mind.

"You love pizza?" I asked, trying to learn something about her.

She shook her head. "Never had before. But when you go so long without something like that you begin to miss it in a new way."

I nodded, understanding that. I never cared for classical music. But as the years went on, I began to miss the classical tunes my mother would play while she cooked large suppers for the pack every Sunday.

For a time, we sat at my dining table with no words to exchange. After a while, I finally worked up enough courage to look up at her.

Our eyes locked briefly until she shifted a glance toward the front door.

"I can leave," she said, as if offering me a way out.

"Where would you go?" I asked with curiosity.

She frowned and looked toward the door with confusion and worry.

"I don't want to hurt you," she finally said in a low tune.

"Why would you?" I asked, knowing she wouldn't.

She grimaced. "I am not meant to be here," she spoke with bitterness.

"Because the man responsible for running the last decade of your life said so? Told you to never trust anyone or let anyone help you?" I spoke harshly.

Danni stood sharply, eyeing the door.

I stood slowly, raising my hands in surrender.

"I'm sorry. I just hate what that man has done to you."

She tilted her head to the side with curiosity.

"Why do you care so much?" she asked. "Your Alpha treats you badly and you stay."

I swallowed the lump forming in my throat. She was right, but how was I going to explain everything? What being in a pack meant? And I wasn't ready to tell her the truth about us. It was still hard for me to believe I'd found a mate. It wasn't something I wanted. My parents loved each other until they were gone within minutes of one another. I never wanted to feel loss like that. But even now, as I faced Danni, it was hard not to look at her and desire to hold and protect her from the one who had turned her.

"Because no one should have to suffer the way you have. And as far as my uncle, the Alpha, it's complicated."

"My life hasn't been that bad," she said casually.

Was she serious?

"So, you chose to fight in pits like the one today?" I asked incredulously.

41

By the look that passed, I took that as a no.

I sighed. "I am offering you a warm bed to sleep in and a place to stay safe. If you run…" I felt myself getting breathless with the amount of emotion crowding my chest. I feared her disappearing on me in the night. I'd only known her for a few hours, and I already feared losing her. I needed to figure this out. "Just, please don't."

Danni studied me for some time, making me feel self-conscious, until she finally nodded.

"I will stay tonight."

That meant tomorrow we'd be having this conversation all over again, but I'd take the win for now.

*

It was still early in the evening when Danni fell asleep. I returned from a shower to find her curled in the corner of the living room on the floor. She acted like a scared animal hiding in the corner. I covered her with a blanket, moving quietly so I wouldn't startle her.

My phone buzzed and I groaned, reading a text from my brother claiming to be outside. News of what happened today had surely spread through the pack like wildfire straight to my brother.

Tanner Lansing had been born in the early 1800's and was a little over a century older than me. He loved reminding me of his role of much older and wise brother. I quietly stepped out of the house, finding my brother's six-foot, four-inch frame sitting up against my fence with his arms crossed over his chest. His light brown eyes glared at me in annoyance.

"I leave for two days, and you manage to be talk of pack all over again. You do realize that our uncle prays for the day you leave willingly or screw up?"

I shrugged. "He can keep hoping and kiss my ass," I snarled. "We both know he was happy when our mom was murdered. He always wanted the pack that he felt was meant to be his."

My brother's jaw popped from the rigid movement he made.

"What you feel doesn't matter. It is disloyal to speak like that."

"As long as I don't go around speaking of a rebellion, I can say whatever the hell I want." I shuddered out a deep breath and looked back toward the house. I wasn't in the mood to be argued with. "I don't have time for this. So, unless you've come for once with something new to say, I need you to go."

Tanner pointed toward my home. "I can smell someone inside. You really brought that animal to your home?" He glared at me in disappointment.

No one mentioned the part about her being my mate. I could see many of them laughing inside, knowing how my brother would react.

"She is a werewolf, just like you and me," I said in a tone that suggested if he spoke of her like that again, I'd bring a little pain into his life he'd never forget. My instinct to protect her was strong and I knew if it came down to it, I'd protect Danni even from my brother.

"Leave," I said, my wolf surfacing.

Tanner glared, confused by my dismissive behavior. "Hey. What is wrong with you? You don't even know that—rogue," he chose to say instead.

I turned to walk back into the house, knowing my eyes were seconds away from flickering gold. When his hand grabbed hold of my forearm, I didn't have time to react as Danni came flying out of the house too fast for me to notice. She moved almost vampiric; with speed I'd never witnessed from a werewolf. I twisted around to find Danni on top of my brother, pinning him to the ground as if he weighed 20 pounds and not 200.

Despite Danni being malnourished and small for a werewolf, it was clear when her wolf was in control the strength she possessed was as if she'd been made to toss anything that stood in her way around like a ball.

I rushed over just as Danni lifted her clawed fingers to strike down on Tanner.

"No!" I spoke briskly. "He's my brother."

Danni paused at the sound of my voice and looked up at me as if checking to make sure she heard correctly.

"I promise you, he wasn't going to hurt me," I said.

"Then, if no one owns you, why do they keep touching you in an aggressive manner?" she asked, not getting up from atop my brother.

"Because, at the end of the day, it is always in someone's nature to be a bully. Especially werewolves. But they do not own me. And no person should own anyone." I felt like she needed to hear that a hundred more times.

Danni gave me a long look and decided to get up. I moved to her side, blocking Tanner from being close enough to retaliate.

"She was protecting me," I explained.

The look on my brother's face was one of shock. I could see he was working through his thoughts to see the piece he was missing.

"Oh, I gathered that," he said. After a minute more, he glanced toward both of us and then his eyes widened, figuring it out. "Is she really—"

"Look! It has been a long day. I think it's best you leave," I encouraged.

This time I knew he'd listen without argument. My brother studied me a minute longer and then turned to leave. I watched him pull away and mentally groaned. My life was about to get a whole lot more complicated.

When I turned to head back, I found Danni a foot closer to me than I remembered her standing. She had a lock of my hair in her hand, sniffing it. She let go and took a step back.

"Please forgive me," she said, embarrassed.

I blushed and smiled. "For what?"

She looked at me as if I should already know why.

"For attacking your brother. I cannot promise it won't happen again. My wolf does things without my say or my understanding."

I shrugged. "He deserved it," I joked. When she didn't smile, I laughed. "I was making a joke. Please, try not to kill my brother."

"Then he shouldn't touch you," she said with a serious tone.

Something told me she would have killed him, or at least tried, if I hadn't stopped her. I realized I needed to take this mating bond more seriously, whether I was ready to accept it or not.

"Let's go back inside," I said.

Danni's eyes wandered about, and I glanced around, searching for any sign of a threat. Instinct told me we were not alone, but I made no comment, walking into my home with Danni by my side.

# Chapter Five

*Danni*

My body had become familiar with sleeping on a hard and cold surface. I hadn't been in human skin for this long in years and the thought of lying in a comfortable bed scared me. There was no chance of this lasting, and the last thing I wanted was to get to comfortable and then lose it all.

Throughout the night I had tossed and turned, sleeping on the floor beside the bed. I could smell Karissa in the next room over and wondered how I could pay her back before she awoke. A thought crept in my mind. I tiptoed out of the bedroom she let me sleep in, making my way to the front of the house and toward the door.

"Already escaping me?" Karissa asked.

I turned, finding her leaning against the wall in a robe. My heart raced, feeling out of place. She seemed so comfortable even though I was a stranger in her home.

I lowered my head and answered, "I owe you a meal."

Karissa walked up to me until we were a few feet apart. "Do you have money?" she asked.

I frowned. "I was going to go catch a couple of squirrels. Or anything nearby," I explained.

Karissa chuckled. "You were going to go hunt for me?"

I'd never been put in this situation. When I was turned, Hansel barely explained anything about what it meant to be a werewolf other than how to serve and be loyal to him. This was new to me.

"I'm sorry. I don't know what is considered proper for thanking you. You fed me yesterday. I only want to return—"

As if sensing my distress, Karissa closed the distance between us, hands pressing into my cheek.

"Oh, I'm sorry. I shouldn't laugh and you don't owe me anything."

I smiled awkwardly, a warm feeling growing in my belly. Her touch was comforting, and I knew I would hate the moment she pulled away.

"I doubt that."

She considered and then nodded. Her hand moved from my cheek, and I suddenly felt emptiness.

"Well, a conversation would be helpful."

"So, you can make a decision on what to do with me next?" I asked theoretically.

"No one is going to harm you," she promised.

I snorted. I'd heard that line before. "I no longer believe in other people's words. I've been promised many things, and nothing promised has ever been fulfilled." My mind flashed back to the many promises my father once kept until he let some stranger take me.

"Okay! Maybe I'm being a bit ambitious in saying that." Karissa processed something and took a step back, wrapping her robe more tightly around her body. "I need to get dressed and then let's talk."

She moved quickly past me and toward the back where her room was. I stood wondering if I should leave and find Hansel.

There was something unique about Hansel that made him able to conceal his identity from other werewolves. He had magic. I'd heard someone call him a witch once but never asked. At the time I barely believed in what I was, after being turned for two years.

The thought of my first shift came to mind and I growled as that memory flooded my thoughts. As a child I'd read comic books and fantasy stories filled with werewolves, but I never imagined them being real. Hansel didn't give me any warning when he showed up in the room he'd kept me in for days and bitten me in his wolf form. I cried for my father as my first shift took over. The pain was excruciating, and I thought I was going to die.

Suddenly, I felt hot and tense inside as if the walls around me were closing in. Chills ran down my spine and taking a breath felt harder to do.

Soft hands touched my arm, and it was like all my fears and dark memories were sucked into a vacuum to be let out later.

I glanced up to find Karissa standing beside me. She held a look of concern that I hadn't seen in years, not since before my life as a human was taken.

"Are you okay?" she asked softly.

I blinked rapidly, unsure of what to say. After several seconds I nodded, still shaken from my memories.

"I need to shift soon," I said.

Karissa gave me a long stare and nodded.

"I know a spot," she suggested, and I nodded.

I was ready to leave, and she could see that. Relieved, I followed her out of the house and off to where I would be free to run.

\*

forward into my wolf's skin. I had to escape her closeness. Not all wolves could shift as fast as me. My family's bloodline was blessed by Fae's centuries ago during a great war between the vampires and werewolves. Many wolves back then were slaughtered simply because of the amount of time it took to shift. My grandfather had done a favor for a Fae and our gift in return was the ability to shift within seconds.

I turned to Danni, standing on all fours, and then shook my body to loosen up my muscles. I moved forward, brushing my white fur against her bare leg, inviting her to shift.

Her eyes widened. "Your wolf is beautiful," she said. Danni shut her eyes and for several heartbeats seemed to fall into a meditational state as I watched her transformation into her wolf unfold. It took her a minute to shift into her black wolf. I had more than 100 pounds on her, but I was also older. One thing was for sure, she needed to build more muscle and gain weight. That only meant having her wolf come out to hunt every day. Without realizing, I was already planning for a future with her. I needed to really clear my head.

I bumped into her body, and she moved out of the way as if politely submitting. I needed to bring enough of her wolf's mind out to get her to follow its lead. Our animal was separate from our human mind but as werewolves we were able to merge and be clear and aware on both ends unless under high states of duress or newly turned. Danni had been a werewolf for nine years and had yet to learn how to merge her wolf's thoughts and instincts with her own human consciousness.

In a playful manner, I bumped into her again and this time nipped at her ear causing her to whine. I knew she was far from being a submissive wolf and wanted her to stop acting like one. It was evident that Danni hadn't found her wolf's true path yet. I'd learned I was a Sentinel wolf within the first 10 years of my life. I'd be in bed and wake up at the age of nine and run into my parents' room to tell them a scary werewolf was nearby. Every role each wolf took was instinctual, but whoever turned Danni seemed to repress her ability to find her true self.

One thing was certain, she was dominant. But as to what kind of dominant wolf, I had yet to figure out.

This time Danni's wolf whined and twisted out of my next playful attack and leaped atop my back. I smiled internally, as my wolf got excited and leaped into a run. The thrill of being chased made my wolf run faster as we played and chased one another for the next hour.

*

*Danni*

I woke up with the sun in my face. Someone warm was pressed against my back, arm draped over my waist. Carefully, I twisted onto my back, finding Karissa asleep beside me. We had run together and hunted as wolves, falling asleep soon after. I'd never had so much fun in my life. Parts of our time shared was a blur, my wolf taking over on occasion, but most of it was coming back to me.

Hansel never let me go outside of his property line on the rare occasion when he did let me run as a wolf. The thought of running free with Karissa again thrilled me. I stared down at the hand at my waist and felt myself smile. Karissa looked so peaceful that I was tempted to curl back against her and sleep longer.

A ladybug landed on her nose, and I watched her sleep unaware, wanting to capture this moment forever. Something about Karissa made my wolf pace all the time. I reached out, lightly pressing the tip of my finger against her nose. The ladybug crawled onto my finger, and I placed it on the ground.

When I glanced back at Karissa, her nose wiggled as if she had an itch. I felt amazed by the simplistic actions she made that moved me. There was something inside of me that wanted to touch her again.

Karissa's eyes popped open as I was about to lean in. She lifted, glancing around, trying to place where we were. I watched her stretch out and found myself looking at her breasts a few seconds longer than I intended. They were round and full. Her nipples were taut from the cold breeze. For a few heartbeats I wished my smaller breasts were as perfect as hers. Karissa was naturally beautiful, whereas I was rougher around the edges.

I glanced back toward her eyes and realized I'd been caught staring. I turned my head away.

Karissa smiled, her cheeks glowing a light shade of red.

"First human thing you've done," she said, hesitantly.

I wasn't sure if I'd made her uncomfortable. "I'm sure you don't need anyone staring at you like that. I'm sorry!" I said, feeling abashed. She was the first possible friend I could have in years and the last thing I wanted to do was jeopardize our small connection.

"You didn't do anything wrong. Don't apologize," she assured me.

I wouldn't question her feelings. I nodded and glanced around, taking in the scenery. There were small patches of grass and bushes around us, with trees at a distance. I took a deep breath, enjoying the aroma of flowers and wildlife all around.

"We should get going," Karissa said, standing up. She brushed off as much dirt as she could and waited for me to stand.

I followed her closely back to her car, where we'd left our clothes. We had been on the other end of the state park, so no humans were around to find us walking naked.

Somehow, I knew this moment shared with Karissa meant more to me than all my old happiest memories combined. With this ounce of freedom, I felt what it meant to live. I hoped to have a few more great memories with Karissa before I had to go back to the only life I'd known for the past nine years.

# Chapter Six

*Karissa*

After getting back to my car, I found text messages my uncle left while Danni and I were running as wolves. I mentally grimaced and considered my options. If I ignored his request, it would only infuriate him and cause Danni to act violently if he came to my home hostile. But I also didn't think Danni was ready to be seen by so many werewolves all at once.

"Are you okay?" Danni asked, shifting her body to face me. She held a look of concern.

I smiled weakly and nodded. I put my car in drive and began heading to the main road.

"Do you always do that?" she asked.

I kept my eyes forward, responding, "Do what?"

"Smile when I can smell your anxiety?" she said.

I opened my mouth only to close it again. I didn't want to lie to her. Not purposely.

"My uncle wants you to come to see him. I don't think you are ready for that," I said honestly, hoping she didn't take any offense.

Danni looked forward as I continued to drive, pondering on my assessment. She suddenly became still and rigid.

"We don't have to go," I said, already sensing her inability to maintain control.

Her fist tightened before loosening. I used my nose and could smell her wolf surfacing.

"Am I a prisoner?" I finally heard her ask.

Thoughtfully, I took a few breaths before I answered her question. If it were up to my uncle and I wasn't bonded to her, I knew Danni would be dead or imprisoned until the Council sent someone down to get her. Due to my claim, she was untouchable unless she presented as harmful to the pack or herself. My uncle was purposely requesting her presence now to put her in an uncomfortable situation in hopes to deem her unfit to be alive or freed.

"You are under my protection," I decided to say. Briefly, I glanced at her before continuing. "You are no prisoner as long as you stick with me," I added. I wanted her to understand the deeper meaning of my statement.

"I see," was all she said. Danni shifted away; her brows slanted into a frown.

I pulled over to the side of the road, hoping she'd open up to me. I knew this wasn't easy for her but if I was going to protect her, I needed to know something. Giving both of us a moment to think, I ran the tips of my fingers in a circular motion of the center of the steering wheel.

"I know you don't know me, but I need you to at least trust me when I say...I have the best of intentions when it comes to you."

"Why?" she asked bluntly.

"Because," I paused, not ready to tell her everything. I took this opportunity to look deep inside myself and gazed up into her eyes. "Because I care about you and I need you to be safe," I responded. I let out a ragged breath, my throat tightening. My wolf saw no concerns, eager to claim Danni, while my human mind felt weighed down by anxiety.

Hesitantly, I reached out wanting to touch her hand. She looked down, seeing what I was doing, but didn't move. When my hand covered her own, we both seemed to relax at the same time.

Every time Danni gazed into my eyes, it felt like she was seeing inside my heart and taking another piece of me with her. Danni opened her mouth but closed it again, averting her eyes.

"My wolf would kill for you," she said adamantly, shaking her head. "And…that is new for me. I don't meet people or get the chance to care." She grimaced and looked back into my eyes. "So, for that, I will do better to try and trust you. Please know that I want to. It's just been years since I've had someone I could trust."

I nodded. "Please! Tell me what happened?" I asked, needing to know for myself and not for my uncle and the pack. I'd only tell him what he needed to know and nothing more.

Danni sat back into her seat and sighed, and I knew it would be a moment before she would speak.

\*

*Danni*

Part of me contemplated getting out of the car and running off, but I knew if I left it would be the end to seeing her again. And the end to the happiness I'd experienced in less than 24 hours. When I found my voice, I also felt more fear swelling at the pit of my belly. I hadn't told my story to anyone before. I wondered if she would want to know the full truth. Deep down, I already knew the answer.

"My mom died when I was eleven. That left me with a father who was unable to express love and kindness. Losing her only made him worse, and he turned to gambling to try and pay the bills instead of working a job." I could see Karissa on the edge of her seat, taking in every word. I wasn't sure if telling her would help the way I felt about everything I'd experienced or hurt me more. I could see she cared and that's what kept me speaking. "I can't remember a time when he said he loved me or gave me a hug. And if he lost a big hand from the money I'd earned, his verbal abuse would shift into beatings."

Karissa reached in and grabbed my hand. I could see her response surprised even her, but I didn't pull away. I froze, worried if I continued, she'd let go.

"Go on," she whispered.

This time, I didn't hesitate to look into her eyes. I felt wide open and unafraid.

"My father placed me under a bet that he lost. At least, that's what I'm told."

"Did this…man ever—" I could tell Karissa was working hard not to growl.

I understood what she was trying to ask. I shook my head.

"The night I was taken; I was locked in a room for weeks until he decided to turn me."

"So, you have been held captive for nine years?" she asked.

I frowned. I didn't like that word. Captive. But that's what I had been. I knew that deep down. Each year that passed I told myself something different. That this life would one day lead me to something better. Maybe I was right if I could stay near Karissa a while longer.

"I fight for him, and he takes care of me."

"No!" she said in a rasped tone. "You have been forced to fight for him or you die!" she said, her fingers now turned into claws, piercing into the steering wheel.

I couldn't wrap my head around why she cared so much.

"Was he there yesterday?" Karissa asked, attempting to hold in her snarl.

I wondered if I should answer. Hansel told me no matter where I went, he'd always be listening in. Somehow, I believed him. He wasn't just a werewolf. He was more. I bit my tongue and lowered my head.

"I promise I will protect you!" she tried to assure me.

I grimaced and shook my head. "Don't promise me something like that." I looked up and faced her with gold eyes. My wolf had been triggered. "I can smell your desire to run from me. You wish you never met me." I snarled and shook my head, knowing my wolf had awoken and spoken for me. I covered my eyes with my hand and sighed. "I have told you. Don't make promises."

Karissa took a long moment before speaking. I felt her hand slip away from mine as she straightened and faced forward. I thought she was done with conversation, but she spoke before putting the car back into drive.

"This is hard for me too!" is all she said.

We drove the rest of the way back into town in silence. I wasn't sure if this was the first stage of failure for us. I could feel the tension radiating off Karissa and knew I was somehow the cause. I looked out the window and noticed the place I was at yesterday. I expected her to pull into the driveway and take me back to my cage. I lowered my head down, sensing my end to knowing her, and sighed.

She pulled into the parking lot, as I suspected, and turned off her vehicle.

"Are you taking me back?" I finally asked after a minute of sitting there.

"Taking you back where?" Karissa asked. She glanced up and sighed. "Oh, no!" She took off her seatbelt. "I wanted to show you something first before we head to my uncle's."

I nodded and got out of the car with her. I was worried she was lying but reminded myself of what I felt deep down. She wasn't my enemy. Perhaps I would tell her everything one day soon. It might be the only way she could truly help me.

We walked back through the main entrance and into the gym to find a dozen wolves lying free from cages atop blankets. Many were bandaged and badly hurt but seemed to be getting proper treatment. There were large water bowls and meat to feed them with.

Three people watched us approach and smiled at Karissa as we walked inside. I was taken aback. I recognized the wolf that Johnson had placed next to me the night of my fight. I rushed to it without a word, kneeling beside its fragile frame.

The wolf saw me coming and growled, afraid I was going to hurt her. My eyes shimmered gold and I lowered onto my stomach, flat on the ground in front of her and pressed my forehead against her.

"It's me," I whispered. When the wolf recognized me, I sighed and felt a tear fall from my eyes. I felt all her pain and wanted to kill Johnson for harming her.

"We live in a cruel world," I told her and ran my fingers over the top of her head.

"Danni." I heard Karissa call out my name. She was standing a few feet away.

I kissed the wolf's nose and slowly stood. When I turned to face Karissa, I was met with three sets of eyes. I recognized the man who was with Karissa when I first met her but not the other two.

"Hi!" The girl who looked a couple of years younger reached out, offering her hand. "I'm Jessi," she said energetically.

Instead of grabbing her hand I sniffed to make sure she wasn't a threat. I'd been too caught off guard to pay attention to the unfamiliar faces.

She smiled and peeked toward Karissa before slowly dropping her hand.

The second woman waved toward me but stood further back, more afraid of me than I was of her.

"I am Amber," she said.

When my eyes landed on the man I saw last night, I frowned.

Karissa waved toward him. "He never got the chance to introduce himself to you," she said.

I moved around her and toward the man, causing the two women to take a few steps back. He held a scent that was attached but not his true odor. It was a familiar scent.

"Everyone calls me Jenkins," the man said, comfortable with my invasiveness.

I took in a deep breath only a few inches from his throat before I lowered it down to the pocket on his shirt. Without permission, I reached in and pulled out a pocket watch.

He pointed and I snarled, immediately slamming my hand against his chest. I watched him fly across the room, dropping onto his back.

Karissa moved swiftly, standing in between me and the two women who seemed to move further away.

I frowned and bit my lip, realizing what I'd done.

"It's okay. Everything is fine," Karissa spoke calmly. "You okay?" she called out to the man, getting off the floor.

I clutched the pocket watch tightly, not willing to let it go, and moved further away from everyone. It been so long since I held this in my hands. I had no desire of it being taken from me again.

"Just got my ass tossed and feeling a loss of pride, is all," Jenkins laughed. "For a young werewolf, you are certainly strong," he said.

I frowned, confused by his reaction, expecting him to come at me. I'd only ever known Hansel as a werewolf. From what Hansel told me, werewolves didn't like to be challenged. Jenkins, on the other hand, brushed off his clothes as if we'd been playing around.

"I forgot about the pointing thing. I'm sorry," he said to me.

The two women began to relax when I acknowledged his apology.

Karissa came to my side. "He wasn't trying to point at you," she said, reassuring me.

"Tell that to my wolf," I said, finding her words pointless. "I don't like being pointed at."

"Fair enough. I'll try not to be so careless again," Jenkins said.

I studied him for some time and frowned. "You are not mad?" I asked.

He shrugged. "I don't get my head twisted in knots over things like this. Not like most dominant wolves. I made the mistake. It's a trigger for you and I understand how that feels." He smiled. "So, let's all keep this between us."

"Deal," the one who introduced herself as Jessi rushed out.

"Is that your pocket watch?" Karissa asked, studying the watch in my hand.

I investigated the palm of my hand and opened it to find a picture of me and my mom right before she died. I kept it close enough for no one to see inside but me.

"I had this with me the night I was taken," I said quietly. "He let me keep it, until the last time I shifted and didn't shift back to human. He kept it in his pocket, promising to give it back one day. Promises!" I sneered in a raspy tone.

Hands brushed my arm and I looked up to find Karissa watching me with sympathetic eyes. I'd been consumed, looking at the picture of my mom and me. It felt so long ago that I saw my mother's face.

"I'm sorry. I looked inside when I found it on the floor," Jenkins said. He didn't announce his conclusion of who was in the picture, but he didn't need to. I knew Karissa could tell by the way her eyes softened.

I wanted to change the subject. I felt too exposed.

"What will you do with the wolves?" I asked.

Amber spoke up in a soothing tone. "Once they are healed and strong enough, we will take them far from civilization and set them free."

I nodded. "They would like that," I said. I glanced to Karissa and could see she was struggling with something. "Thank you for taking care of them," I told her.

"Like I said, no one deserves to be caged." Her eyes held mine firmly. I knew she was right, but it wouldn't change the outcome of what Hansel had planned for me when he took me back. We gazed up at one another for some time until the silence was broken.

Jenkins cleared his throat, distracting us. "So, shall we head to see the Alpha?"

I continued to glance at Karissa, knowing my fate was in her hands.

"Only if you want to," she said to me.

"I don't," I spoke adamantly. I saw her look of worry and sighed. "But I can feel that I must, for you."

Karissa sighed in relief, but I could still sense an underlining dread.

"Then we should go. I've kept him waiting long enough."

I nodded, wondering if I'd be locked in a different cage by the end of the day.

# Chapter Seven

*Karissa*

We made it to the house I'd once considered my home. When I lost my parents, I had lost this place too. My uncle had done a lot of remodeling and I hardly ever wanted to come here to see the change he created.

The energy here was all business. A place for the pack to meet and discuss things, topics ranging from finances to gaining my territory. I parked the car on the street and turned off the engine. The nearest houses were more than 100 feet from us. We had thick bushy trees and a six-foot gate that went around our land to uphold our privacy. Between the house itself and backyard, we had almost one acre of property. The house was two stories with a basement.

My mom had built this home over 300 years ago. Once I looked at this place, all my memories came flooding back to me.

Soft hands pressed against mine and I gazed up into her eyes. My heart raced as my pulse bounced in my ears. Just like that, she was able to pull me out of my pain.

I hadn't realized I was crying until she reached across and wiped a tear from my cheek. Instinctively, I felt the need to fall into her arms. It was a werewolf's need to connect through touch. But it was Danni being my mate that made me crave her touch specifically.

"I wondered why I saw concern in your eyes," she spoke softly. Danni looked toward the house and sighed. "This is hard for you too. I see that now."

She'd used the words I said to her earlier in the car, after our run and hunt. It meant a lot that she'd paid attention to my words. Despite her own emotions, she'd listened to my thoughts.

My heart drummed even harder at how caring she was. There was something unique and exotic about Danni that I wanted to explore despite my fears. It was the kind of beauty seen few and far between.

Danni's knuckle wiped away another tear and I smiled, feeling relaxed. She took me by surprise when the tips of her fingers slid into my hair. I shut my eyes, soaking in this moment. How could she take my mind away from all the anxiety I had when coming here? We had barely known each other a day and already I wanted more of her.

There was a knock against my window that startled me. Both Danni and I looked toward my side window, finding my brother standing there. I couldn't read his expression, but I knew him well enough to know he was worried for me. I knew what he was thinking. Out of all the people to end up mated with me, it had to be a woman like Danni that could bring danger to the pack. I thought the same thing at first but, at this point, I no longer cared. She was my mate, and we would need to eventually figure out what that meant for us. First, I needed to tell her. I had been hesitant, not sure if she would be able to handle or even comprehend my words.

I opened the door and stepped out of my car. Tanner scanned me thoroughly, searching my eyes briefly as if he feared an unseen change. I chuckled and shoved him away, disinterested in his hovering.

"I am fine," I spoke calmly. If I sounded anxious, Danni would know and be on higher alert.

I turned to find her hesitant to step out of the car. A few pack members stood atop the front patio of the house, scrutinizing and judging Danni from a distance.

"Walk away!" I growled, giving them a threatening scowl. My need to protect her was just as dangerous as Danni's, and I wouldn't allow anyone to antagonize her or me. It was always members of the pack that had originally come with my uncle when he took over as Alpha who seemed to test my patience.

The few that were standing around huffed, heading into the house. I could sense at least 20 of my pack were here. I hoped Jenkins warned them about Danni's triggers or this day wouldn't turn out in our favor.

It was mid-day, with a lot of time to cover. I stared up to the sky, trying to find the right words to comfort Danni or we'd be here for a while.

"You shouldn't keep—"

I waved my brother off. My uncle was the least of my concerns. I skirted around the car and opened Danni's door slowly. Hoping she'd trust me enough, I offered my hand. I could see her contemplating.

I wanted to choose my words carefully. "I have your back. Always!"

For the first time, I heard Danni chuckle softly. She took my hand, allowing me to assist her out. We stood at eye level, inches apart.

"Always is a strong word to say and another way of promising."

I grinned, wanting to hear her laugh again.

"What if what I'm saying is my truth to you? And I'm someone who means what I say even if it's a promise given. What then?" I asked softly.

I never expected her to respond but she surprised me again.

"You haven't given me a reason to doubt you. You deserve more than just my trust. I'd have to be inclined to start believing you, even if it's a promise."

I blushed and nodded, looking away before I could say anything else. How were my feelings for her growing so fast in such a brief time? My mom would talk to me about mating bonds and how intense and quick everything would feel. Part of me thought she was exaggerating but now I realized how right she was.

We walked up the porch into the house, ready to face my uncle together. More of the pack lingered near the front, cautious and curious about Danni. They kept their distance, for which I was grateful.

We found my uncle sitting at the far end of the table when we stepped out into the backyard. We'd had a long wooden table that had been with our family for centuries, seating more than 12. My auntie, Elaine, sat at the corner end next to my uncle and placed her glass down when she noticed us.

"Karissa, honey!" she chimed out with excitement. She was my aunt through her mating bond to my uncle. I was thankful to have her in my life. She felt more blood related than my uncle, always supportive of me. Her smile was warm and inviting.

I hadn't realized Danni and I were still holding hands until I had to let go. I didn't leave Danni's side, allowing my aunt to come to me as she embraced me tightly. She gave me a quick kiss on the cheek before turning to Danni with a wide smile.

"And you must be the young woman who everyone can't stop talking about," she exclaimed. "I never thought my niece would find—"

"Thanks for inviting us to lunch. Sorry we couldn't come sooner," I said, cutting my auntie off. I gave an expression that she'd read from me too many times in the last 20 years.

My auntie smiled, understanding what I was trying to say. "That's okay. Your brother told us you two went off hunting. I'm sure you are famished."

I smiled and nodded. "I'm fine." I looked to Danni who seemed ready to run out at any moment. I knew my aunt was full of energy and always smiling. That could be a lot for someone like Danni, who had been experiencing the opposite reactions from people for a decade. I was positive even long before that too.

"Would you like something to drink?" I asked her, already suspecting the answer.

"I'm fine," she said with a quick nod. Her body was stiff, and I could smell her wolf on edge.

At the end of the day, we were here for a potential interrogation. The last thing I wanted to do was prolong our stay.

I looked back toward the table, acknowledging more of my pack. Dean was seated closer to the end to where we stood, smiling toward the both of us. My aunt walked back to sit beside my uncle, who I was not interested in facing right away. Jenkins approached and sat next to Dean. It seemed everyone my uncle wanted out here was present. I noticed that excluded my brother, not that he'd risk status for my mate or me. Tanner loved me, but we had different definitions of taking care of the ones we loved. I looked to Danni and then walked to the empty chairs that were far from my uncle and right across from Dean.

We both sat at the same time. Even though Danni was oblivious to the mating bond, I knew what she needed for us to get through this interrogation. Discreetly, I pressed my hand onto her lap and gently squeezed, allowing some of her anxiety to flow through me.

Danni took in a needed breath and shifted a furtive glance at me. I could tell my touch confused and soothed her all at once.

"How was your night?" my uncle asked. I could feel his eyes on me and didn't look at him right away. Instead, I took in the ambiance. A few tall trees made the backyard appear more forest-like. Other than the patio deck we sat on, the rest was just grass. My mother's garden that used to reside along the walls of the home she built was now gone. It didn't look like this backyard was ever used for anything more than pack meetings. Being here, seeing all the change, was a slap to my face.

It was Danni's turn to comfort me. Openly, she reached out and placed her hand atop mine that rested over the table. I could sense all eyes focused on our linked hands. Danni was fierce, not feeling any pressure from their gazes.

"We can go," she whispered to me in a soothing tone.

"Actually, you can't. Not until I get the answers I need," my uncle said, dismissing Danni's words. He was Alpha and therefore meant if he wanted us to stand on one foot, he could make us. Or at least try.

His harsh tone was all Danni needed to hear to stand up sharply. Her eyes were simmering gold and her fangs were exposed as her face partially shifted. The bone in her jaw popped, Danni staring my uncle down like he was a threat that needed to be put down.

Everyone stood but stared with shocked amazement, except my uncle. Jenkins glanced briefly at me, mentally telling me to get Danni under control. If Danni attacked my uncle, Jenkins would have no choice but to defend him and kill Danni if he were ordered.

Danni was still holding my hand with no intention of letting it go. Her body was still, like a predator right before a attack.

"Danni," I called out in a whisper as I stood, brushing my other hand up her shoulder. She needed to feel my touch. It was the only way to bring her back to the surface. The last thing I wanted was this meeting to turn violent and for my uncle to condemn her as a threat to the pack. But part of me also wanted to let her speak. I'd never had someone fight for me this openly. Already, Danni was protective of me in a way I never imagined.

My brother would make suggestions toward my uncle anytime an issue arose, but never in a way that made it clear that he had my back first. I didn't blame him. My uncle was also Tanner's uncle and Alpha. And Jenkins was under my uncle's leadership long before he met me. But within a day, I'd found the one person who would truly stand for me, and it made me want to cry. Not that I planned to, especially now. This was what being mated meant. Choosing each other first before anyone else. Trust and honesty. And from there, love.

Danni's chest caved in and out rapidly. "Karissa says it is your duty to protect your territory and pack. That is what makes you an Alpha." Danni looked to me for confirmation, and I nodded.

"Does being Alpha include caring for all…in your pack?" she asked my uncle.

He sneered. "Yes, but you are not in my pack," he countered, finding her question irrelevant.

"You remind me of someone…" Danni's words drifted off for a second as if she were captured in a memory. When I squeezed her hand, Danni straightened her posture again. "I am new to understanding all of this. But listening to how you speak to one that is of your pack and blood… where I have been, that is called being a cruel and narcissistic Alpha."

The Alpha stood slowly, heat radiating from his body. Both his hands curled into fists, pressing against the table.

"I don't care if you have the makings to be an Alpha. You are years from that if you even make it that long." His eyes shifted to me as if I'd known what her wolf status was the entire time. No dominant werewolf, especially one so young, could partially shift. Only an Alpha or one that holds the potential of being an Alpha could do so. "You are in my territory and came uninvited. Why shouldn't I overlook a few minor details, and have you killed?"

Everyone's eyes widened at his threat.

"Christof," Elaine jumped into conversation. "Forgive me for speaking out of turn, but a bond like theirs isn't a minor detail." Being a wife to an Alpha like my uncle, she was allowed to interject in discussions but even she had limits. My uncle never liked being questioned openly.

My uncle knew if he tried to have Danni killed, I would be forced to kill him, or at least try. I was beginning to realize my uncle would go as far as to kill me for justifiable reasons, if that meant getting rid of me.

I stiffened and kept my wolf under control as I spoke. "You know I love this pack and as long as you remain Alpha, I can't do anything but wait for someone else to outrank you," I said honest and openly. I wasn't threatening him, only stating a fact.

He snarled but said nothing.

"She did not come here willingly," I stated, changing the subject. Danni was on edge and we needed to end this conversation soon.

"Oh, and how did she arrive?" my uncle asked with sarcasm.

I looked to Danni, who stared back at me with hardened eyes. Her wolf was still partially in control. She could understand what I was asking and nodded.

I would only share what he needed to know. "She was kidnapped and turned against her will at the age of fifteen."

"My goodness," my auntie said, baffled.

Jenkins had not known the truth either and slowly sat back down in dismay. It was exceedingly rare for a young teenager to survive a werewolf bite.

Dean's expression held no surprise. He knew whatever Danni's history, it would be one of harsh realities.

"Go on," he encouraged.

"The werewolf who turned her has been keeping her..." I chose my words carefully, knowing what could trigger Danni and heighten the tension. "Forcing her to fight in illegal fighting pits." I sighed when Danni stayed calm and continued. "When I finally announced myself to the werewolves responsible, they all scattered, and she was left inside of the cage as you witnessed."

My uncle contemplated my words. I could see him working hard to find a way to discredit me, but with Jenkins there as my witness, there wasn't much he could say, and he knew it. It didn't mean he wouldn't try another way of trying to run her or me off.

"Since you did your job, then there is no reason to keep her around. She is unpredictable and must leave my territory."

"No!" I stated and held his eyes firmly. As a Sentinel wolf I had the ability to look any Alpha in the eyes and confront them when it came to the safety of a pack. "The leader of that fighting ring was someone I forced out of our pack several months ago. He doesn't find our authority frightening enough."

"That is your problem and not—"

I cut my uncle off. "Now, it's my problem when you've been trying to prevent me from being Sentinel since you got here." I snorted, bemused. "I told you we needed to capture and hand him off to the Council, and you dismissed that and told me to chase him off instead. Now he thinks he can dip in and out of our territory with no consequences. How many others will begin to do the same because you can't seem to put your foot down with rogues?"

My uncle slammed his fist into the table hard enough to hear a crack.

"Your continuous undermining is what wears me out more than those fucking rogues." He moved as if to come toward me but stopped when he noticed Danni shift her posture, ready to lunge if he took another step. His eyes hardened but he stayed still.

"He will come back and probably with more friends and the person who had been keeping her for the past nine years. She is not only bonded to me, but under my protection," I said firmly. I knew I would need to explain a lot to Danni when we left. She deserved to know how bonded we were and why my uncle made the comment of her being a potential Alpha. I was still processing this all for myself.

"It is law, and it is her right," Dean agreed with me. He looked to me. "As long as Danni does not harm any in our pack, she has the right to walk within our territory." With Dean as mentor, it would be hard for my uncle to go against his words without factual proof.

"Fine. But a wolf with no control will slip soon enough. I only hope it doesn't cost one of your pack's lives," my uncle added.

I smirked. "And I hope you stay out of my way, or those rogues will cost us more than a life," I retorted. I heard him snarl but I turned and walked toward the sliding door with Danni at my side. I knew his hatred for Danni in his territory and desire to get rid of me wouldn't go away. There would be a next time and we'd need to be ready.

*

*Danni*

After leaving Karissa's uncle's home, we went out to shift for a second time today. Any time I was wounded and bitter inside, Hansel would leave me caged to hold in my anger for the next fight I'd be heading to. His way of assuring our victory. No wolf could live caged and be normal once set free. Definitely not a werewolf.

When my wolf finally slept, I shifted back to human skin and looked at my kills. I had ended up catching a doe and two squirrels before my wolf was satisfied. I sniffed at what was left and smiled.

"Pleased with yourself?" Karissa asked, walking over and handing me clothes. She looked down at the kills I'd made. "We can leave them for the animals to finish off," she said. "We can come back out tomorrow morning."

I looked up and took the clothes. There would be a tomorrow. I thought after the incitement I displayed with Karissa's uncle, she would change her mind and cast me out of her territory. It was only fear making me think that way.

"Hey," Karissa whispered, kneeling beside me. "I meant every word to my uncle. You are under my protection."

I thought hard and long, thinking of everything that was said and looked up.

"How are we bonded?" I finally asked. Those words had been said, and I couldn't ignore that. Since laying eyes on Karissa, I'd felt a connection to her but clearly there was something more.

Karissa averted her eyes.

"Unless we are only bonded because you helped me and my wold listens to you," I said, not wanting to know the truth. "Am I staying with you out of some sort of…" I thought carefully of the right word. "Obligation?" I ended.

A distant look passed through Karissa's eyes and before she could say anything, she stood up quickly into a guarded position. A low rumble echoed from her throat. She sensed a threat close.

The hair on my arms raised. I sniffed the air and caught his scent right away. It was Hansel. My muscles tensed, fearing that my time with Karissa was about to end. I could feel him inching his way closer and this time I growled without realizing it till it was too late. I'd never growled at Hansel before. I covered my mouth as if that would stop me, but it didn't. My wolf peeked through my eyes and narrowed in on his location. Somehow, I knew where he was and knew he was staring straight at me too. My heart drummed erratically in my chest. If he attacked Karissa, I would attack him, and he could sense that.

As if air was forced back into my lungs, I took in a sharp inhale when I sensed Hansel leaving. There was no doubt he would have attacked Karissa if he didn't sense me as a threat too. He was expecting me to back down like I'd been doing for the last nine years. I learned quickly never to attack him. And if it were anyone other than Karissa I would have stood back and let him take me again. But there was something about Karissa that gave me a dire need to protect her. I feared the consequences of this moment when the day would come that Hansel would take me back.

"You knew who it was," Karissa said in a knowing tone. I hadn't realized she was now staring at me.

I could either lie or be honest. As far as I knew, Karissa had been honest with me from the beginning. I'd been keeping things from her. Things I was still not ready to share, but this I could be honest about. Her life was in danger and for that she deserved to know.

Slowly, I stood and got dressed. I stood barely an inch over her five-foot, seven frame and nodded.

"That was my…"

Karissa continuously preached that no one should be owned but that's what I'd been. Owned. Property to Hansel. As much as I told myself many stories, I knew that as the truth deep down.

"The werewolf who you've been under for the last nine years?" she finished for me, sensing my emotional troubles.

I lowered my head and nodded. Fear was coursing through me. "I shouldn't have done that," I blurted.

"Done what?" she asked.

"I growled at him. I've never—" I paused and then glanced into her eyes. "But I couldn't let him hurt you. Your safety is worth any consequence he gives me in the future."

Karissa's hand reached out, cupping my cheek. "He won't get the chance to touch you again." She saw my eyes shift gold and grimaced. "I know, I know," she chimed out. "That sounded like a promise." She was about to speak again but smiled instead. "Let's head back to my house. I'm sure you are eager for a shower."

I smiled and nodded. "A bath, actually."

Karissa chuckled. "Yes, a bath. And then we can talk about everything," she assured me.

I could be patient. Following her lead, I lingered close to her side, ever so watchful of Hansel reappearing when we least expected. When we made it back to the car, I sighed in relief and smiled inside knowing I'd have another day with Karissa Lansing.

# Chapter Eight

*Danni*

"If you need anything just shout out my name," Karissa informed me, her eyes hesitant.

She handed me a towel and I stepped into the bathroom and nodded, my attention on the hot water in the tub. I took in a somber breath and placed the towel on top of the toilet. There was an aroma coming from the water that was fresh and soothing. I tried to place the scent, but I was unfamiliar with it.

"Tea tree and rosemary." A blush formed over her cheeks. Karissa pointed to the tub as she clarified. "That's what you're smelling. It's great for your skin and calming."

Absently, my brows crinkled as a warm feeling began to settle inside my chest. Peace.

"Thank you," I whispered, watching her head out of the bathroom.

Once the door was shut, I began removing my clothes and walked the short distance to the tub. It had been so long since I'd bathed in a tub or with fresh hot water. Hansel would always hand me a bucket of freezing water and a towel anytime I was in human skin. Just another one of his many ways of reminding me of how small I was in his eyes. The last three years, I'd lingered in my wolf's skin and been allowed to run off and hunt, finding a small pond on his land to soak in. It was better than the days he'd splashed me with water before a fight.

Something warm dripped down my cheek and I inhaled softly, exploring my emotions. A tear that reminded me of how hard my life was. For so long I felt helpless and small but with Karissa, she made me feel significant. I'd lost so much time caged and afraid. The thought of having this night as my only chance to experience comfort scared me.

I slid into the tub and leaned back against the surface. The more I thought about the years I'd lost, the harder it was to contain my emotions. Trying to shake myself out of this haze, I took in a deep breath and submerged. I held my breath, thinking of my time with Karissa. Her eyes were easy to look at, her hands strong yet soft to the touch. I released a breath when my head lifted out of the water and ran my fingers through my wet, coiled hair. For the first time in years, I wouldn't rush or worry. Closing my eyes, I leaned back letting my body relax as I let myself feel content.

*

*Karissa*

There was a connection between Danni and me that seemed to be growing despite the anxiety of giving my heart to someone, but it wasn't something neither one of us could control. I could see the confusion in Danni's expression every time she stood up for me. So many times, since Danni entered the bathroom, I wanted to go in there and hold her tightly. I could feel her tear as if it were sliding onto my skin and into my soul. I could acknowledge that

Danni wasn't like all the other women I had known or dated over the years. It wasn't merely because of what she'd been through. It was more than that. She was different and someone I could already depend on in such a brief time. My wolf trusted her wolf and woman.

Gingerly, so not to disturb her, I moved away from the bathroom, giving her the privacy she needed. I knew Danni had to be questioning her life and if she would ever be able to escape the man who had taken her as a teen.

My phone buzzed. It was a text from Jenkins regarding my uncle wanting to speak to me privately. My uncle was smart and malicious when he wanted to be, and he knew he couldn't get away with talking to me how he wanted in front of Danni. He was an Alpha but lacked the desire to give true orders when it came to those outside of our territory, and I had made it clear to him I wouldn't back down. In his mind, if you didn't acknowledge the rogues, there were no rogues to deal with. It was a foolish philosophy. And when it came to Danni, there was a ferociousness about her that he would never own and that intimidated him, though he would never admit it.

I mentally groaned and slid my phone back in my pocket, deciding to ignore my uncle's request for now.

"Karissa," Danni called through the door.

As if being called for something life-threatening, I moved toward the door within a half second, nearly bumping into it. What was happening with me? My wolf felt frenzied by the sound of her voice. My wolf whined, wanting to claim Danni as her mate. If it had been up to my wolf, she would have by now.

I shook my head and responded. "Yes?"

"I—" there was hesitation. "Could you..." her voice drifted away again.

Sensing that she wanted me to come in, I opened the door. I tried to look everywhere but on her. Her dark-skinned complexion was revealed in the water. Her hair was wet, water dripping down her face.

"I know this is a bit much to ask," she said awkwardly, knees pinned up to her chest, her arms crossed over them, hugging herself.

This time I did looked into her eyes, my heart drumming in my chest. I felt as if my lungs could collapse by the mere sight of her. I needed to get a grip on my mind and flushed skin.

"Nothing you ask will ever be too much." I sounded pathetically breathless and smiled, trying to not feel awkward.

She nodded, oblivious to my aroused state of mind and held out a sponge. "I haven't had my back washed in years. Since before I was taken. I just want to feel it…at least once," she said in a delicate timid tone.

Something so small meant so much to Danni. I walked over and rolled my long sleeves up to my elbows, sat on my knees, and grabbed the sponge from her hand. I hunched over the tub, dipping the sponge into the hot water. It was warmer than what humans could handle, and I wondered, *when was the last time she took a warm bath?*

Danni shut her eyes and waited as I moved my hand over her skin, running the sponge from the nape of her neck to her mid back. My pinky brushed against her skin and my heartbeat quickened.

"My mom used to do this when I was little," Danni admitted. "When she died, I lost that. That sensation of being soothed." Danni sounded relaxed.

I'd been holding my breath when Danni's words were absorbed by my mind. My eyes had been trailing wherever the sponge touched her skin until now. I stopped and stared at the wall tile above the tub, thinking of my own childhood.

"My mom would play in my hair every night before bed," I mumbled. "To feel that comfort again." I'd never shared that with anyone before. Never talked to anyone about my parents until now. Not even my brother. It felt amazing and scary to share, but I didn't regret it.

Danni's fingers slid through my hair, and I inhaled softly. Water dripped down my face from her wet fingers and I didn't bother holding back a tear. Is this what I'd feel for the rest of my life if I allowed myself to be happy? Hopeful and open to all possibilities and love? I let Danni's fingers linger in my hair, shuddering as chills swarmed my back all the way up to my neck. My wolf pleaded for me to let Danni in. Two wolves meant to be mated and held back by human thoughts were bound to explode in our faces.

Our eyes eventually met. The gold in Danni's darkened and I knew my eyes matched hers. The bathroom steamed as if we were the source of heat.

"I feel drawn to you. More than I can explain or understand." Danni spoke softly as if trying to sort through her feelings aloud.

I bit my lip, knowing that I needed to tell her the truth. Explain what was happening between us. I shut my eyes, regaining some focus. If I didn't leave this bathroom soon, my actions would speak louder than the words I needed to say.

"There's a lot I need to explain to you," I said, mentally hating myself for ending this moment between us. "Once you are dressed...we can talk."

Danni nodded. I could see she was nervous.

I reached up and brushed my knuckle against her cheek. "Nothing's wrong."

She gazed into my eyes and sighed. "I'll be out in a moment."

I stood and nodded, heading to the door.

"Karissa," she called out. I turned and she smiled at me. "Thank you."

I grinned. "Back at ya."

Out of the bathroom, I headed into the kitchen in need of a beer. Opening the fridge, I pulled out a bottle and took the wired cap off with my bare hands. Everything inside me wanted to kiss Danni and begin something we couldn't take back. But there was a lot of issues to address. My uncle would do everything in his power to not accept Danni into his pack. And her being a potential Alpha who also didn't respect his authority was the justifiable excuse he could use. But there was another issue to address. Me. Before meeting Danni, I promised myself I would never open my heart to being mated. Having a mate meant the possibility of losing one. And Danni clearly had no experience being in a relationship.

There were a lot of odds against us, and Danni had her own battles to face.

Danni walked into the kitchen, wearing one of the tank tops and sweatpants I let her borrow. No! I wouldn't be able to let her go. Just seeing her in my home, I knew my wolf had found its mate. The fear was real but so were my feelings for her, despite what I was trying to avoid.

I smiled, awkwardly. "Do the clothes fit?"

Gingerly, Danni ran her fingers over the cotton fabric of the shirt.

"Fits well enough," she said.

I knew that was a lie. Her shoulders were broader, making the shirt tight around her chest, but she'd never complain. "We can go to the store tomorrow after our hunt," I suggested, trying to distract myself with normal conversation.

She shook her head in protest. "No need," she said.

"Why?" I asked. She lingered near the hallway while I still resided in the kitchen, using the island counter space as a barricade to keep from being tempted to close the distance between us.

"You've already done more than enough," she answered.

I felt myself frown before I realized the emotion building in my chest.

"I'm not going to let him take and cage you again."

"I believe you think that." Danni said, now staring off in a direction nowhere near me.

Instead of blurting out words that I knew would be out of anger, I gulped down half the bottle of beer before setting it down. If this afternoon had taught me anything when I felt the presence of a werewolf, it was that Danni's captor wanted her back. Another thought came to mind.

"I can't sense him," I stated.

Danni looked up and frowned.

"What?" she said, confused.

I cracked my knuckles and sighed, frustrated that for the first time I couldn't sense when an uninvited werewolf was in our territory. There was more to her captor but after years of abuse, I could not fault Danni for not sharing any details of him. He'd made sure to teach her that lesson first, I was sure of it.

"I am a Sentinel wolf." I explained what that meant and my abilities until Danni seemed clear enough to understand my upcoming questions. "That's how I found the illegal fighting pit."

Danni sighed, looking away from me. She moved across the living room and peeked out of the window.

"What are you asking me?" she whispered. There was fear in her tone. She moved to another window, looking out as if searching for someone.

The sky was darkening and other than my intrusive brother I wouldn't get any unexpected visitors tonight. I had motion detector cameras around my house to watch out for humans or other beings that tried to enter my property. Not having lived in the pack home since my parents' death, I didn't have immediate back up if someone threatening came knocking.

"The man who had been holding you against your will for the last nine years was within 100 yards of us this afternoon, and I didn't sense him. I also felt a presence here last night and that's only because I could feel someone lurking, just not what or who. So, I guess I'm trying to ask you, why can't I sense his presence and exact location?"

Danni's body stiffened before twisting and locking eyes with me. "Perhaps its best to just let him take me back. Then I won't be around to cause you any more trouble with—"

"Don't do that. Don't throw yourself under the bus to protect him." I knew my words were a bit harsh. Danni averted her head and turned to look back out of the window. I could hear her wolf snarling, wanting to be free, but Danni had been crippled by this man's power.

I couldn't take this distance anymore. I needed her to understand. Being mated was about more than finding a forever partner. And if she knew what was happening between us, she'd let herself feel what was true and be honest with me and herself. She was no weak wolf, but her captor conditioned her mind to think like one when it involved him.

"Please, look at me," I asked, softly.

She hesitated but eventually turned to face me.

"I can't see you suffer at the hands of him, physically or emotionally," I said. "Just like you wouldn't be able to see me suffer by his hands."

"Or your uncle's," Danni added, a growl laced in her tone. "He would kill you. I can smell that desire from him."

I was not surprised. I knew my uncle too well and as a Sentinel wolf I had the ability to see through his bullshit more easily because it was my natural duty to question things that made no sense. And because Danni was a potential Alpha, she could smell his desires. Only an Alpha could sense the intent of another Alpha.

Part of me hadn't processed that not only was my mate lost and dangerous but was also a potential Alpha. To be mated to an Alpha held a lot of responsibility and when Danni finally grew into that role, she'd be a force to reckon with.

"I know," I said. Closing the distance between us, I reached out and grabbed her hand. "Maybe if I share something with you, it will help you see the value of opening up to me."

"You mean about us being bonded?" she asked.

I nodded.

"So, it is something deeper?" she questioned.

I nodded again and smiled. "Much deeper."

*

*Danni*

Having been guided to the couch, I sat beside Karissa taking in her nervous smile and excessive foot tapping. Whatever she wanted to share with me was important.

I pressed my hand over her thigh to get her to relax and found myself not wanting to move my hand away. She wore shorts so my fingers were brushing her soft skin and it took everything inside me not to run my fingers further up her thigh. What was happening to me? I'd never had an inappropriate thought in my life but then again, I never had this much freedom to feel this way.

When I lifted my eyes up to Karissa's, I found her staring down at my hand on her thigh and quickly moved it, believing I'd done something wrong.

"I'm sorry. I..." I didn't know what to say, struggling to speak.

Karissa cleared her throat, cheeks turning a shade of red. "It's fine. You didn't do anything wrong."

"But you look uncomfortable," I questioned.

"I'm..." Karissa immediately closed her mouth as if she were about to say too much.

I gazed at her, confused. "You're what?" I countered.

She smiled. "Never mind."

I turned my body from her and frowned. Clearly, she wasn't comfortable enough to be honest. Seconds past and I felt like my time with her was running out. I'd be a fool to think I could last another day with her at this rate. Hansel would come for me again and I would do the right thing and let him take me.

"Danni! You didn't do anything," she tried to convince me. I heard her sigh aloud as she spoke in a tone that suggested she was nervous. "I liked it. I was aroused, okay!" she said, shifting her head away in embarrassment.

"What?" I looked up, even more confused.

"Your touch. I liked it." This time her eyes did not waver from mine.

I took a moment to process that and my own feelings. That's what this was. Me having feelings for her, despite my blindness. I'd never had time as a young girl to have crushes and after Hansel took me, life was too dark to think about anyone in any other way than hatred. But here I was for the first time, happy to be near someone and touch them. I had an old friend as a kid who was gay, but I never considered my own sexuality. Is that what I was feeling now? A desire to touch another woman? I'd been taken as a child but that didn't stop me from growing up with the desire to be loved one day. If anything, I had dreamed it for too many long nights.

Karissa watched me with nervous eyes. I didn't want her to think I didn't feel it too, and I smiled at her with reassurance.

"I've never had a connection like this before." I looked into her eyes before drifting my gaze down to her lips and suddenly I wanted to see how it would feel to kiss her. I'd been so swamped with adjusting to this unexpected change that I hadn't considered what my feelings were underneath. "I feel like I'm constantly at war with myself but hearing you now, I can admit it's hard being near you and not touching you. I don't remember seeing anyone with another person and having such an urge to touch like I'm constantly feeling. I'd kill for you. And I know that shouldn't be something anyone romanticizes but that's how

I feel. Sometimes I feel out of control by the thought of anyone else going near you."

Karissa nodded, another blush stretching down her neck. "Being a werewolf with feelings is a lot different than being a human."

"How do you mean?" I asked.

"Have you ever had a crush on someone?" she asked.

I shook my head. "I don't know. I mean...I would see a person in my class and think they had a pretty smile, but that's about it."

"So, you never explored or learned enough about the kind of person you'd like?" Karissa asked.

I could tell where she was going with this conversation and laughed. The sensation was still new to me, but it felt good.

"You mean...did I ever explore if I liked girls or not? No." I said, honestly. "But just because my life hasn't given me the chance to explore those kinds of things doesn't mean I'm too broken to know what's happening. I just didn't realize what this was until now."

Karissa eyes narrowed. "You're not broken."

"I know you don't think that."

Karissa smiled. "You know why I believe that?"

"Why?" I asked.

"Because, if you were broken, we wouldn't be having this conversation," Karissa explained. "You'd be closed off and unable to comprehend what you're feeling, and you seem pretty damn self-aware."

She had so much confidence in me. I considered her words. Maybe she was right, and I was hearing Hansel in my head telling me I was weak and not worth saving.

"I've never hoped before. But that's all I've been doing, since meeting you."

Karissa reached for my hand, linking our fingers together. "I have told myself too many times not to let anyone make me feel what I'm feeling now."

"Why?" I asked.

"Because…" Karissa smiled. "The thought of giving myself to someone and losing them scares me."

"Like your parents?" I asked.

She nodded. "That pain and heartache was unbearable to witness. I can't take that."

"I don't believe that." I had more than enough confidence in Karissa's ability to face challenging times, but I understood. "The thought of leaving and never seeing you again terrifies me. Part of me knows you're my only hope to freedom but not at the risk of putting you in danger. And you shouldn't have to carry my hardships."

"Danni, I know you don't like when I make promises, but I meant what I said. I have no intention of letting anyone take you." Karissa squeezed my hand as a tear slid down her cheek.

I reached out, brushing my thumb against her cheek. "I cringe less every time I hear you use that word."

Karissa smiled. "It's more than us being werewolves." She let out a long breath. I sat silently, giving her a chance to explain, the palm of my hand lingering along her jaw.

Karissa shut her eyes for a few heartbeats before letting out a sigh.

"The way you are beginning to feel for me, and I for you, that intensity has little to do with us being werewolves and more to do with what we are to each other." She spoke quickly as if nervous to say everything on her mind.

I pulled away, trying to understand. "Then what are we?" I asked, knowing there was a lot more to this. Karissa hesitated and I realized she wasn't ready to say whatever this was. I was still living in the possibility of Hansel taking me back again. There was no point in saying anything if it wouldn't last.

"He has magic," I blurted out, changing the subject. I wanted to give her something honest since she'd opened her home and even part of her heart to me. When she was ready to tell me everything she'd been holding back, I hoped I was still around to listen.

"What do you mean?" she questioned.

The tension between us was broken as she waited for me to explain. My palms felt sweaty from the thought of Hansel listening in from a distance.

"The one who took me," I admitted. It was becoming easier to say the truth of my past nine years aloud. "He has magic. Someone once mentioned him being a witch."

Karissa's eyes widened. "Witch." She leaned back into the couch and snorted. "That makes sense. I thought for a minute I was slipping on my skills."

I looked toward the front door as if expecting Hansel to burst in at any moment but when he didn't, I sighed in relief. I hated how much power he had over me and hoped when the time came to face him, I wouldn't give in so easily.

"Thanks for telling me," Karissa said.

I nodded. I was happy I'd told her. Karissa needed to know because when Hansel came for me, I didn't want to leave her at a disadvantage. I glanced toward the door and stood, giving her a genuine smile.

"Your friend is coming. I will give you some space."

Karissa stood and frowned. "I don't smell anyone."

"He's a mile out." Karissa looked at me dubiously and I realized she couldn't sense him yet. "I guess living in my wolf for 3 years made my nose stronger."

Karissa's furtive expression left me to wonder if there was more to my ability to smell someone so far out. "You don't have to disappear."

"No, I think it's wise to give you two some space. Besides, he has a habit of pointing and I don't want to lose control. Not tonight." I took my leave, heading into the room she'd provided just as a knock sounded at her door. I walked toward the window, staring out at the dark sky, and sighed, sliding down the wall. There was no comfort from lying in the bed and I didn't want to grow to like it when this wouldn't last. Part of me knew I was stronger than I was forced to believe but I didn't know if I was ready to take the steps to regain my freedom. That meant facing Hansel and he wasn't anyone to challenge easily.

I curled my knees into my chest, resting my chin against them as I let the silence swallow my thoughts. I could worry later.

# Chapter Nine

*Karissa*

I offered Jenkins a drink, but he declined, taking a seat on the couch. He looked toward the bedroom where Danni was, skeptical over what to say openly.

"She's not listening." It was obvious that Jenkins wanted to speak privately and somehow Danni had known that, judging by her offer to leave. I could tell Jenkins didn't believe that whatever he needed to say wasn't going to be overheard and I frowned. "Trust me, okay? Say what you need to."

Jenkins nodded, running the palms of his hands over his jeans. His brows kneaded together before relaxing with a deep sigh.

"I don't know how to say this without betraying your uncle's trust."

I knew what he wanted to say, and I wouldn't make him feel obligated to tell me anything if it meant jeopardizing his status with my uncle.

"You don't have to say anything," I told him, sitting beside him. I smiled sincerely, showing him I wasn't mad. "We've been friends since you joined this pack, but I never forgot that you were loyal to my uncle and you would never go against him. And I would never put you in a position to do so."

Jenkins sighed in relief. "So, when you say I don't have to say anything, is that because you understand?"

I patted his leg. "I understand," I said clearly. "If my uncle showed me anything today...it's no love. And that makes me expendable, especially if it gets Danni out of this territory."

Jenkins tensed awkwardly; lips pursed in deep thought.

"What?" I asked. There was something else on his mind.

"Have you ever once considered, if you would have accepted your uncle into the pack as our Alpha, there wouldn't be tension between the two of you?" Jenkins looked at me, waiting for an answer.

I rolled my eyes and snorted.

"I'm being serious!" he expressed.

I bit the inner walls of my mouth, trying not to be insensitive. Whether I understood or not, Jenkins looked up to my uncle. There were times I wanted to see what he saw but I knew the truth and would always trust my instinct.

"I did once. Before you were in the picture. Before then, I admired my uncle. Anytime Christof came to town, I thought he was gold even with my mother's annoyance toward his presence."

Jenkins sat quietly, not moving an inch. I had never shared anything about my past with my uncle.

"But I was still learning a lot and didn't get fully involved with pack business until 50 years ago. And then I witnessed the greed and selfishness he possessed. How much he lusted and envied my mother's position as Alpha over their father's pack. But you are just his loyal friend. And a man. So, you can't see what every woman does anytime he steps into a room and tries to belittle us with just his presence."

Jenkins eyes faltered for a heartbeat. I reached out and squeezed his hand.

"I don't fault you for being blind. Just don't judge me for being able to see," I said honestly. I stood and walked to the door. It was time for him to go. I wasn't mad at him for questioning my distrust in my uncle, but it stung a little to know that part of him thought it was my lack of trying that created all this tension. "At the end of the day, I stay for my pack and from here on out, I will do what's necessary to keep my pack and mate safe." No matter how many times I talked myself out of the idea of having Danni as a mate, it didn't change the fact that she was. I couldn't turn her away even if I had a gun to my head.

Jenkins followed me to the door and turned to face me, standing outside. "She can get you killed."

I knew he was afraid of losing me, so I kept in my anger that was resting at the base of my throat.

"And my uncle can get this entire pack killed, or at least torn apart." I grunted, dropping my eyes as I thought of what to say next. I loved Jenkins and nothing would ever make me distrust him, but he still had a lot of growing to do too. "Would you have questioned another man in our pack over his loyalty to his mate? Told him to turn her away because of the risk to loving her?"

Jenkins eyes widened, realizing the discriminatory statement he had made, and I could see remorse.

I sighed. "I don't know what my future with Danni looks like, but I do know I won't turn my back on her. And I will not sacrifice her to keep my place in a pack with an Alpha who is unworthy. She is my mate. The sooner my uncle accepts that, and anyone else who has a problem with it, the better it will be for everyone."

Seeing the expression of annoyance on my face, Jenkins didn't say anything else and left. I shut the door louder than I intended, hand gripping the doorknob as I breathed out slowly. Jenkins wanted me to be the one to tap out, as if I would ever consider that. Tapping out meant allowing my uncle to destroy, piece by piece, everything this pack once stood for as well as get Danni killed.

Soft hands brushed my arm and I turned to find Danni beside me. Her eyes were filled with care, and I watched as she lifted the palm of her hand up, pressing it against my chest. I could feel the vibration of my fast-beating heart as we listened together in silence.

"I didn't listen, but I felt every moment," she admitted.

My vision blurred briefly from the tears she pulled out of me. How could she bring out so much of me when I spent years trying to put walls up around my heart? My eyes lingered on hers until I dipped my gaze down to her lips. When my eyes made it back to hers, she was smiling.

"I like you, Karissa Lansing," Danni said confidently.

I smiled, taken aback by her bluntness. Despite being held captive and made to feel like someone weak, Danni displayed more openness and emotions than anyone, including me. The least I could do was be brave like her.

"I like you too, Danni." I said the words and it felt right.

"Simmons," Danni said.

"Excuse me?" I replied.

Danni smiled. "My last name is Simmons."

I smiled and out of instinct I pulled her in for a hug. Danni's arms closed around me, not too tight and not too soft. I stifled a moan when she dug her nose into the crook of my neck. She was a wolf that led with her nose, and I was glad I didn't have an issue with her sniffing me.

When I pulled away, I told myself not to blush, though one was creeping up.

"I suppose you haven't seen a movie in ages," I exclaimed, needing some momentary distance.

Danni laughed, shaking her head. "Not in a very long time."

For some reason, I wanted to give her the most normal night possible, filled with junk food and movies. "Then you are in for a treat."

*

*Danni*

We'd fallen asleep on the couch, watching movies until the sun crept up. It was the first time I'd slept on something soft in years. I would have slept on the floor if it wasn't for Karissa falling asleep against my shoulder. I never wanted to move, watching her sleep until my eyes closed.

Karissa's head had made its way down to my lap as she lay curled on the couch. She looked peaceful and it wasn't something I wanted to disturb. Gently, I ran my fingers through her hair. The longer I stayed here, the harder it would be to leave. I wasn't naïve and knew this couldn't last.

The curtains were open, the sun brightening the living room. Tightness began to squeeze my lungs, and I looked out the window in the front of the house. I knew it was him. I recognized his scent. My wolf clawed inside, wanting to fight to protect Karissa, but I wanted to crawl into a dark cave and hide. Across the street Hansel stood, unbothered by my internal conflict. He believed he'd dominate me again, and he looked forward to the day he reminded me of my place. Beneath him.

Our eyes locked and my breath caught. My jaw tightened, knowing he was using his magic to compel me. He wanted me to kill Karissa and join him.

I shut my eyes, tears forming as I exhaled slowly. It was as though Hansel had slid inside my barriers and forced a response out of me like I was his puppet.

The fear of Karissa being harmed sliced through his magic and I shouted, "No!"

Karissa's head jolted when she sat up. Immediately, as if we were linked, her gaze went straight toward the window. Her eyes widened and it was obvious she wanted to go out and kill him.

I gripped her arm, stopping her from standing. "Don't!"

Karissa looked from me to Hansel in bafflement. "He's right there, lurking like a stalker. I just want to speak to him." I let her go and she stood, storming her way to the door.

I followed quickly, nervous and unsure of how this would end.

We stopped short of Karissa's fence. Hansel casually walked across the street and stopped on the sidewalk. He grinned, trying to pull one of his charms on Karissa that I knew wouldn't work.

"It's becoming increasingly annoying that I can't detect you," Karissa stated, crossing her arms over her chest.

"Ah. I have a few tricks up my sleeve," Hansel replied, eyes looming over me. "I'm sure my child has expressed her opinions on how I am able to escape your Sentinel abilities."

He'd been here last night and overheard. He looked at me with disappointment and annoyance in his eyes.

I lowered my head instinctively, as I had done many times when I knew I was in trouble.

"She is not your child," Karissa retorted.

Hansel grinned. "Seems you know everything," he said, displeased.

"I never shared—"

Hansel cut me off. "We will address your poor behavior later."

"I will say this once. Leave my territory now or the next time I find you here, I'll kill you," Karissa threatened.

Hansel's tall, lean build tilted forward as if taunting Karissa to act irrationally. "Not without what belongs to me."

Karissa took a step forward, her bravery and defiance toward Hansel making me temporarily speechless. She snarled, fighting the impulse to lunge.

"She belongs with me," she clarified.

Hansel leaned back, eyes shifting between the two of us. He didn't speak for a long moment, processing something I'd yet to understand. When his expression formed into a wide grin, I knew whatever connection I had with Karissa was special.

"Ah. I see. Hmm." He pressed his thumb and index fingers over his chin, going into deep thought.

"You only have one chance to leave in peace," Karissa said. "I will do what's necessary to keep you out and her with me."

"How about we let her choose," Hansel offered.

My eyes darted to him before shifting toward Karissa in confusion. This was a test. If I chose him, I knew he'd punish me severely and I would never get to see Karissa again. But if I chose Karissa, he'd eventually snatch me anyway and go after Karissa so I wouldn't be able to run back to her. Furthermore, I could put her through so much trouble by staying.

"I would like to hear Danni tell me to leave," Hansel grinned, expecting me to go with him.

"I know what you're thinking, but I know how to defend myself." Karissa repositioned, facing me but still having a good defensive stance in case Hansel attacked. "The last thing I want to do is make you feel like you must choose. I know, no matter how dark life's been, he has a hold on you that only you can break." She reached out, linking our fingers. "All I'm asking is that if you choose to stay, it's because you no longer want to be controlled by him. Not for me, but for you."

"Danni. Come home," Hansel called out.

I stared at the ground, contemplating my choices. She was right. No matter what choice I made, it had to be for me first. But I could also admit to myself that I couldn't picture life without her after knowing her for just a day. Was I only fascinated by Karissa because of her act of kindness or was there something more?

"But I also want you to stay. I want you to fight. I want you to choose you," Karissa added.

My eyes brightened. I knew if I stayed, this would be the first step to facing my past. There had been so much time lost being his puppet, fighting in cages or killing other werewolves in his bidding.

"Would it be wrong to stay because of you too? I want to be free for me. But also, to be at your side."

"Be wise," Hansel warned. I could tell he was getting nervous. After all, other than Hansel's magic, I was his muscle. Losing me would weaken him in some way. But I wasn't foolish. Hansel had many aces up his sleeve and was very capable of killing someone himself. "Her pack will never accept you. Especially because you are a prima Alpha in the making."

I had no clue what that meant but I'd heard Karissa's uncle Christof say that about me. Everyone had looked nervous seeing me partially shift when he'd called us to his pack.

There were so many troubles to face on both sides, but the one thing that haunted me the most was losing Karissa. She was right, and I trust her to know she could defend herself.

I glanced at Hansel, finding courage I never owned toward him. But fear crept back in as I looked at Karissa. The harm he could cause her and her pack. I didn't want to risk her well-being. Part of me thought it was better to never see her again rather than witness her death, but I had to make a choice.

"I choose…"

Karissa's eyes lingered on me, hope dangling in them. She didn't say anything, giving me the freedom to choose.

With her, I'd always be free.

"I choose to be with Karissa," I said, looking straight into Hansel's eyes.

First, there was shock. Hansel couldn't fathom me choosing Karissa over him. I watched as the corner of his eye twitched. But soon, shock shifted into anger and bitterness. How much energy and time did he put into grooming me to do his bidding? And all of it had been wasted. Hansel wasn't someone who handled rejection gracefully. He believed I was his and that was all that mattered.

"I'll give you a day or two. Live in your fantasy," Hansel encouraged, though there was no happiness in his tone. "But know, when I take you, I'll have to kill her as a lesson. Nothing personal."

"Leave," Karissa held her place with no fear or hesitation. There was only a calm eeriness in the way her wolf stood at the surface, ready to fight and kill if she must. Her fingernails elongated into claws, a signature of how hungry she was to fight him now.

Hansel cocked his head to one side, inquisitive and scrutinizing. When he straightened his spine there was something new that I'd never seen in his eyes. Patience.

In the years being under his control, Hansel had been anything but patient. He needed things right at that moment, nearly costing me my life for him to have them. The thought of his time being wasted brought out a rage within him in which I'd constantly been in the crosshairs of. But now he stood calm and patient, like he'd learned a new life lesson. Clarity. He would wait. But for what, I had no clue.

He smiled. "You'll come back to me."

His confidence made my wolf pace inside. She didn't want to go back. My wolf would fight even me to avoid ever going back.

I watched him turn from us, not worried Karissa would give into her wolf and attack. He slid both hands in his front pockets like a bystander passing through, turning the block as he walked away. I could no longer see him, but I felt him. Felt his laughter and mockery. He was treating me like a rebellious child who'd run away and come home when I realized life was worse without him. I didn't want him to be right.

"He's gone," Karissa whispered. She moved to my side, hands along my arms. "He won't come back," she said.

I nodded. "I know. He will wait for me to come to him."

"But you won't," Karissa snarled. Her eyes lingered, wanting me to agree but I couldn't.

Today I'd agreed to stay with her but who knew what tomorrow held.

Karissa sighed and nodded. She wouldn't force me to answer.

"Let's go inside," she said.

I nodded and followed her to the house I'd grown familiar with. How long would this last? Was I kidding myself? I hoped not.

# Chapter Ten

*Karissa*

My wolf forced me to wake from my sleep, body springing forward in bed. I panted and sniffed, trying to find the scent that had caused my wolf to wake.

After meeting Hansel for the first time, I'd been on edge for most of the day, Danni and I sticking close to the house. We'd ended the night with dinner and a movie until I'd been ready for bed.

My eyes adjusted to the dark. There were no uninvited wolves concealed in the shadows of my room, but there was one within my pack's territory. He was young and newly turned and by his scent, he was from here. That was new. No human was turned within our territory without the Alpha's direct consent. Even then, there was a screening process. A step I would have been involved in as Sentinel.

I slid out of bed, dressing quickly. There was a knock at my door.

"Come in."

Danni stood at the entrance. "I can feel you stirring inside."

"There is one newly turned wolf in my territory. I must go check it out." Then reality kicked in. I couldn't leave Danni here alone. I didn't trust she'd stay, and I feared Hansel might take it as an opportunity to take her if she was alone. Or my uncle.

But Danni's mind had already been made up. She had on the new shoes I bought her with loose denim jeans and black V-neck shirt. I'd braided her hair into two sections down both sides of her head the night before. She looked ready to go.

I grabbed my own shoes from the closet along with a katana I took on certain occasions. I'd learned to fight with swords at a young age from my parents. They'd lived in a time where swords were needed and when it came to facing an enemy that lived centuries. They still used them as a fighting tactic, and I needed to be ready.

I called Jenkins on the way to the car, telling him to meet us at a club. It was a human club that was known as a hangout spot for drifters and runaways. The city should have shut the place down ages ago when a runaway teen girl was found there, drugged and nearly assaulted.

Whoever the two new wolves were, I doubted they understood what they were, or they wouldn't have gone to the club. Newly turned wolves couldn't handle crowded places. All it took was someone bumping into them to rile their wolves up enough to fight. And fighting led to shifting which led to killing.

It took us fifteen minutes to get to the club. I parked illegally in an alley across the street. It was too busy to find decent parking close enough and I didn't have time to care about the city rules when lives were at risk. I kept my katana inside, not wanting to draw attention to us. Danni and I walked across the street.

Jenkins met us at the front entrance of the club, his smile gentle. I knew he was being cautious since our last conversation.

I patted his shoulder. "We're good," I assured him and smiled.

He acknowledged Danni, who'd been standing at my side, quiet and eager. This would be a new experience for her.

"You're looking sharper than ever!" Jenkins was taking the initiative, accepting that Danni was not going anywhere. That meant a lot.

Danni only nodded, her eyes on the door of the club.

I whispered, "Follow my lead," and she nodded.

"There are a few more werewolves inside. They have your scent," Danni muttered.

She was right. I sniffed and frowned. Three of my pack were inside; they knew they weren't allowed to go into human clubs.

"I guess I'll be doing some reprimanding too!" Jenkins whined. He didn't want to go through with reporting this, but it was his duty to inform the Alpha and make sure they were punished. My brother was normally in control of punishing undisciplined wolves. As Beta, second to an Alpha, he held a lot of responsibility. But in the last several years, my uncle had sent him off every chance he could. My uncle never liked anyone feeling too close to his position.

Tanner was strong and old enough to challenge my uncle for the position of Alpha, but what my uncle didn't understand was that a wolf who didn't have the Alpha power inside could not maintain the role. It was imprinted in us from day one of our wolf's birth, who we were and were going to be.

But any wolf who had lived as long as my uncle, knew that a wolf could appear as strong as an Alpha, but it didn't mean they were ever meant to be one. Something I doubted he ever was. There was a reason my grandfather had skipped his eldest son and given the Alpha status to my mother.

"Ready?" Jenkins asked.

Danni had seen her share of clubs and crowded people surrounding her in a fighting pit. She didn't need to be educated on what to expect from the sounds, smells, and behaviors of others. But there was a difference for her tonight. She wouldn't be the one all attention was directed toward and that gave her some relief.

I took the first step and opened the door as the sound of contained music blasted into my ears. Sweat, mold, vomit and other foul odors whiffed up my nose and I blew out a breath, the mixed smell forming a bitter taste on my tongue. I checked to see how Danni was doing and she seemed unbothered. I was sure she'd smelled worse.

A bouncer sat on a stool, giving the three of us curious glances. He was dark skinned and bald in the middle of his head. His black polo shirt fit tight over his bulky body, a small flashlight in hand. Most of the people here tonight looked barely twenty-one and rowdy. We didn't fit the image.

"ID's," he asked.

I knew there were teens in here and he was giving us a hard time. He probably thought we were cops.

Danni didn't have an ID so I knew I'd have to talk my way in here without resorting to violence. I ran my index finger over my bottom lip, scrutinizing the crowd. It had to be over 300 people in a club that fit maybe 200. And this was only the first floor.

"You really going to ask for our identification?" I questioned.

The bouncer frowned but found himself uncomfortable when he tried to make eye contact. He briefly glanced at Danni and Jenkins before giving me his attention again.

"It's policy that I—"

"Then you should do that for every person that comes through," I countered. "Look," I knew he was nervous, not sure why he was being timid with us and acting like we were tough cops making his night hard. "If you're worried about us being cops, we are far from it. We're only here to find one individual and then we're gone."

The bouncer pursed his lips, and I waited to give him a chance to make the right decision. He didn't want to risk his job if we were cops, but I knew he also didn't want to find out what happened if he told us no.

"Be quick," he rushed out and waved us through.

I smiled and walked in, Jenkins and Danni at my side. The bar counter stretched over twelve feet long, and every inch filled with customers looking for their first or next rounds of drinks. It amazed me how much money people threw away at a club on drinks alone. There were high-top tables at every corner with a small dance floor and a DJ high on a platform, playing hip-hop music. People were scattered everywhere, drinks in hand or on the tables, sticky and wet from spilled alcohol.

"This way." I nodded toward the stairs leading to the basement from the back. We skirted around tipsy people swaying to the music. Three young men rushed up the stairs, trying to race each other and I stepped to the side before motioning down.

By the neon lights flashing and music twice as loud as above, I knew the basement was where all the main action happened. I peeked before making it completely down the steps, seeing a large stage centered against the wall and a bar alongside it. There were dancers giving the crowd what they wanted, money being tossed to the floor. Mostly everyone stood; there were only a few tables placed along both sides of the walls.

"Is this the life I've been missing out on?" Jenkins asked. He didn't need to shout. Our werewolf hearing was exceptional.

I shook my head. "Go on and when a drunk person throws up on you, don't get mad. Comes with the life."

Jenkins snorted.

"Not all places are the same. But this place," Danni said, inspecting it. "This is as bad as it can get in a human club."

"Did you have to fight in human clubs?" Jenkins asked.

I was about to tell Danni she didn't have to answer but she surprised me.

"More than I cared too," she growled. "I'd be caged in the back, forced to hear this chaos pounding in my ear. And by the time all the mundane patrons left, the dance floor would turn into my bigger cage to fight in. By then, I'd be so riled up it wasn't hard for me to rip into a wolf. But I fought more werewolves caged like me than regular wolves. There's more of us out there than you think."

I knew she had to be on edge now, reliving the anxiety of waiting to fight. The sound of loud music pounding in her ears and chaotic behavior. I reached out and squeezed her hand. It was brief but all she needed. We'd be out soon.

"I can smell him," Danni said. "He's in the bathroom. His wolf is pacing."

I nodded in agreement. "They probably realized something is wrong with them. The music and wild energy feeding their wolves' potential frenzy."

There was a line forming along the wall outside the men's restroom. Jenkins noticed members of our pack huddled in a corner; his expression became grim when they noticed us first. Jenkins pointed to the stairs, and they scurried out without either of us saying a word. It was a problem we'd deal with later.

"Restroom's closed." I shoved my way to the front, a burly man over six feet five inches turning and posturing. If he thought that would make me back down, he was mistaken. I pointed my thumb over my shoulder. "Find the restroom upstairs."

He huffed, irritated I'd even suggested. But before he could make a comment, Danni snarled and showed her canines.

He jolted backward, taking a few steps.

"What the fuck?" he said. Unable to meet her glare, he twisted and shoved through the crowd on the other end, spilling drinks as he left.

The other men seemed to get the message without seeing whatever Danni had done.

"Nice!" Jenkins chuckled. "I should have tried that."

But he couldn't. Only Alphas or potential Alphas could partially shift. And she'd done it faster than any Alpha I'd ever seen, her face now back to its human features.

"We try to keep the humans ignorant to what we are," I said as more of a suggestion.

Danni shrugged. "You know how many times a human witnessed me shift in and out after a fight? They don't want to believe, so they don't."

This wasn't a discussion I wanted to debate here, so I tabled it for later. Drawing my focus back to the door, I knocked once and opened it. Jenkins stood guard, directing anyone that approached toward the restroom upstairs.

There was a man washing his hands, heedful of another man pacing along the corner of the wall.

"You should go!" I encouraged.

He turned off the water, shook his hands and reached for a paper towel while motioning to the door. Eager to leave, he didn't bother reaching for another paper towel when the first one slipped from his fingers.

"That guy's tripping," he advised us on the way out.

Danni followed me inside, quiet and watchful.

I was great at finding uninvited werewolves and fighting them if need be but talking them down typically required an Alpha's touch. If he shifted, I wouldn't be able to force his shift back. But an Alpha could. So, I had to be delicate and not push him.

The restroom wasn't big, just two urine stalls and one regular toilet hidden behind closed doors. Two sinks resided diagonal from the urinals where the strange new wolf paced.

Playing safe, I kept my distance giving the man a chance to notice us. He was too consumed in battling for control. If he had lasted this long without having his first shift yet, I was impressed. Calling him a man wasn't exactly accurate. He looked barely legal. He had a babyface that made him look younger than what he probably was, and he was thin. By the clothes on his back, he had to be a runaway.

"You seem like you need help." I was stating the obvious, but it was the only thing I could come up with to get his attention.

He blew out a harsh breath, finding my statement half-witted.

"I'm not interested in foreplay. Please go!" he warned. His eyes never left the ground. But his curiosity to see us kept his head swaying up for a few seconds at a time.

I sighed and tried again. "See. I'd love to leave, but I can't. Not without you."

His chin lifted, spine straightening as he processed my words. It was his wolf. The young man that been human had lost the battle. His glare was cold and deadly, his wolf lip curled with anguish at my uninvited arrival.

"I'm not going anywhere with you." His tone was threatening and guttural. If not for his wolf's growls, the young man's voice would have come out soft.

"You were bitten by a wolf, right?" I pressed. At this point, there was no pretending ignorance was bliss. The sooner he realized the change in him, the sooner he could take back control.

His eyes widened, wondering how I knew.

"Look, I'm here to help. But I need you to come with me. Being here isn't safe or smart." I was attempting to be more suggestive, so he felt like it was his own decision. But the look of distrust and resistance in his eyes told me I'd have to force him out.

"I don't think I want to leave. It's loud and too many people. Too many smells. I'd lose it the moment I stepped out of this restroom," he snarled, pointing to the door.

I could feel Danni's heart racing as she maintained what little control she had. I took a breath, relaxing my shoulders, and felt Danni's tension ease. She was feeding off my own anxiety.

"If you stay in here, you might do something you will regret later," I said, calmly.

113

The young man lifted his head higher, defiant, and challenging.

"Make me."

His wolf was looking for a fight. And before I could say anything, he moved to attack. I was ready but Danni didn't give me a chance to knock him unconscious.

Danni moved with unnatural speed, curling her arm around his neck, and jerking him backward. At his back she lunged and bit into his neck. Blood spilled from her savage bite and the new wolf shuddered before dropping to his knees, not bothering to fight.

I moved to stop her, but I stopped when her eyes found mine, realizing her wolf was in control and not trying to harm him. Danni's wolf was dominating his wolf, getting him to submit within seconds.

Her mouth pulled back from his neck and she stood, letting him fall to the side in shock. The wolf inside him was now asleep, leaving only the young man in utter confusion.

I rushed to the side, grabbing paper towels to cover his bite mark. I didn't want blood dripping everywhere. After a minute, I checked and noticed his bite was already closing into small scars.

I frowned and stared down at his neck. Normally, as a werewolf we could heal completely. But a scar could only be considered markings made by a wolf attack, by silver, or by an Alpha claiming a wolf as his or hers. Is that what Danni had done?

Danni was oblivious to her potential. She looked down at the young wolf and offered her hand. He hesitated, exchanging glances between us before accepting.

The new wolf tried to pull his hand away, but Danni held it tightly, leaned forward, and sniffed him.

"Did a man by the name of Hansel take you in?" she asked suspiciously.

He kept his eyes down at her shoulders, confused but aware he shouldn't look into her eyes. No wolf could stare into an Alpha's eyes without risking an Alpha's wrath. He nodded. "Yes. I was panhandling and he walked up, offering me a place to lay my head. He said his daughter was taken and wanted to help me in memory of her."

Danni's eyes lit up like a campfire. Dark amber and smoldering. As if Hansel had suddenly entered the room, her courage and strength gradually dissolved.

I hated seeing pain and conflict in her eyes. Taking the attention off Danni, I stepped forward.

"What's your name?"

"Randell." His voice was soft.

"Well Randell, I'm Karissa. And this is Danni." I held my hand out. "I want to help you. But you must want to help yourself too."

He turned to Danni for guidance, and she waved for him to follow my lead. He took my hand, and I sighed in relief, mouthing *thanks* to Danni, and opened the door. We walked out calmly, ignoring people as much as we could.

By the time we were out of the club and to my car, Randell was finally able to take a decent breath. I opened the door, and he climbed inside without argument.

"I'll meet you at pack," Jenkins said, walking to his car.

Danni and I stood in front of the car, her eyes piercing into every person who walked by. Her body was rigid and guarded.

I frowned. "What are you doing?"

Danni twisted, grabbed me, and pulled me to the concrete. Our bodies slammed against the hard surface as arrows whistled over our heads, silent enough to not to have the humans notice but deadly enough to cause a great deal of harm. We'd been standing in the alley, out of view from most walking by.

Jenkins rushed back to us, aware of our current state of danger.

"Stay back. Hide!" I ordered, Danni and I crawling to the car. Another arrow nearly pierced into my chest. Danni yanked me on top of her. She laid on her back and I stared down at her, amazed she'd saved my life twice.

It felt nice, feeling our bodies pressed together. But since someone was trying to kill us, I had to focus my thoughts. I twisted off Danni, noticing the silver arrow stuck in my car tire.

"Fuck!" I hissed.

Werewolves didn't use arrows.

"I need to make sure."

"He's dead," Danni said, before I could finish my words.

I shut my eyes. "Double fuck!" Danni had seemed aware of the threat before it happened. We'd saved him from turning and walked him to his death. "Where are they?" I leaned on her to keep us alive.

She nodded. "Two humans. I recognized them. They work under Hansel. Very capable, especially with the help of his magic."

She pointed to the van parked across the street. It was grey, with chipped paint and tinted windows. I looked everywhere but couldn't find them.

"Where?"

"They are hidden by magic," Danni explained.

Jenkins had scared the humans away that been walking toward our path and was now crouched low, 30 feet from the van alongside the same corner. He used a car as a shield, peeking around to spot the threat.

"We need to move from this spot," I suggested. Our backs pressed against my car. We sat like two caught rabbits in a snare.

Danni didn't respond right away. I whispered, "You hear me. We need to move." Our shoulders were pressed together, and I bumped into her to get her attention.

I grabbed Danni before she fell to the ground. I was too focused on the human hunters and their precise aims to realize she'd been hit, probably when she first brought me to the ground. I should have been more aware and smelled her blood.

But now I was acutely aware of blood pooling underneath Danni's unmoving body. I tried shaking her awake. She grimaced and moan from the pain, but her eyes never opened.

Though the arrow had gone straight through, she wasn't healing. I lifted her shirt and saw a gaping hole in her lower right abdomen, just below her ribs. Blood seeped from her wound.

Silver was deadly to a werewolf if it lingered in our bloodstream, but the arrow had long passed through Danni. She should have been healing by now. It was faint but I smelled wolfsbane, a poisonous plant deadly to werewolves and rarely found.

I'm sure Hansel had no intention of killing Danni and the arrow had been meant for me. And Danni had known that too, risking her life to save mine.

There was no way of stopping the bleeding and the poison would continue to work its way through her system, shutting down all her organs and eventually killing her. Wolfsbane also bound the wolf inside, preventing a shift. In many situations, a shift meant life or death. There were only two ways a werewolf survived wolfsbane, either by an Alpha forcing a shift or by magic.

I knew giving Danni to Hansel was a bad idea but so was giving her to my uncle. I felt as if I'd slipped into a new trap that neither of us were prepared for. I scooped her face into my hands and pressed my lips firmly against her forehead.

"I will protect you," I promised.

My wolf cried. A loss of a mate before having the chance to bond with Danni's wolf would destroy both my wolf and me. It was what I'd feared. Taunted by my parents' untimely deaths, I pictured being alone, always aching and needing a mate who would never be beside me.

Soon, my wolf would set herself free and hate the world as much as I did at times. Hate the cruelty of loving only to lose. Be taunted and mocked with possibilities only to have that dream snatched from my grasp like a malicious demon pretending to be an angel.

My snarls continued to grow and whatever rational behavior I possessed slipped from me.

There was no control. No thinking about if a human saw me. No fear of repercussions. My mate was dying and the only way to save her was through the two who'd harmed her and trapped us in place. I twisted to my knees. Another arrow was caught by my hand and tossed to the side. The silver burned my fingers, but I felt nothing but my rage.

I couldn't see the humans, but my wolf would find their scent. Feel their flesh tear between canines. Feast on them without regret.

There was no time to remove my clothes. I snarled, tears flooding my eyes. My shift began, bones breaking, muscles twisting to new shape, and jaw popping as my wolf howled, announcing to every wolf in our pack that I was angry and about to hunt. To kill and feast on humans undeserving of life. I wouldn't regret it. My wolf would never allow me to.

I shook my white fur, standing on four legs. My sight sharpened and my ears perked up, alert and aware of two humans breathing. The smell of hatred and fear. The humans hated what I was but had taken a job from one. I didn't care. They were afraid now and that made my wolf smile.

I glanced at Danni one last time as Jenkins ran toward me. He knew to protect her with his life. A car skidded nearly off the road as I leaped into the street.

The van's headlights beamed on, and I heard the engine ignite as the two human hunters slammed the doors. My head swerved in their direction, and I watched them. Tires skidded along the concrete street and sped forward right at me. I leaped onto the sidewalk, a group of humans startled and tumbled backward in their drunken states. I twisted and turned, chasing the van.

My wolf wouldn't let them get away. I was faster and would wait for the perfect moment to attack. Several blocks from where we'd been attacked, the van made a sharp turn onto a two-way highway and that was the opening I needed to not be disrupted in my kill. My wolf was long and lean, with a strength not many had wolves in their lifetimes.

I ran along the van, finally able to see the humans. The magic had worn off. The man peeked out the side window, eyes widening upon seeing that I was still next to the van. Before he could swerve into me, I used all the momentum I had and leaped, slamming my body into the van.

At first it only shook. But the driver had been caught off guard and then it wobbled before swerving. The van tipped over, sliding 30 feet along the highway before going into the grass and flipping over once, ending upside down.

It was dark for the humans but perfect for me. One of the men reached for a gun, sticking his arm out to point his weapon at me.

I darted to the side and watched his arm shift back and forth, trying to find me. Like the predator I was, my wolf pounced, biting, and tearing his arm off. His hand stuck out from the side of my mouth, gun dropping to the floor. The van was wide enough for me to stick my head inside and clamp down around his shoulder, yanking him out.

The blood coated my wolf, dripped from my canines, and soaked into the soil as I tore into him. His human ally watched in horror, too terrified to try and run. He watched and I feasted savagely.

By the time my eyes looked back into the vehicle, he'd passed out from blood loss and fear. The need to kill him was strong, but a car door alerted me I was no longer alone.

My uncle walked up to me, along with my brother and several members of the pack. My eyes darted to every pair of eyes I could find, searching for the one person who mattered.

The look of disdain and pity was in my uncle's eyes.

"Jenkins has taken her to pack home," My uncle said, closing the distance between us and stared down at my kill. "Hm." There was satisfaction in his smug expression.

"Not as faithful to the laws you aim to preserve as you thought."

I'd killed a human, against a law created by the werewolf council long ago. A forbidden act punishable by death. My wolf didn't care, but my human brain was finally turning back on. I stared down at the human. Limbs torn from his body. Organs spilled from his abdomen. I'd broken a law I'd never picture breaking, and my uncle finally had the means of getting rid of me permanently. And as much as I knew I was in trouble, I looked back at the human pleased with my kill. I didn't care.

# Chapter Eleven

*Karissa*

We made it to pack home, and I went straight to Danni's side. She was sprawled out on the ground outside. My uncle hadn't provided her any comfort and failed to heal her from the wolfsbane in her system.

I dropped to her side and tears fell with me. My hands shook and I found myself bending over her unconscious body, pressing my lips against her forehead.

"Help her," I pleaded. If it had been me in danger, I wouldn't have begged but I couldn't lose her. Despite all the emotional distance I wanted between us to prevent myself from feeling this agony, I'd still found my heart and soul tangled with hers. She was mine. My mate. I needed her. My wolf couldn't survive without her.

My uncle enjoyed my groveling. He'd waited years for this moment. To see me break. Where he took satisfaction, I saw sadness. We were blood and had once been close. But his greed about being Alpha had been the knife that tore us apart.

Everyone stood behind their Alpha, a mix of emotions. Most carried sadness for me, while a few that were loyal to my uncle were pleased to see me weakened. My eyes shifted to my brother. He wanted to help me but would always be loyal despite his personal feelings. He hated my uncle just as much as I did, but would never go against him as long as he was Alpha. As for Jenkins, I watched him struggle to act too but he'd be foolish to speak on my behalf. My uncle would punish him severely if he tried.

I would not hate him for it. I would not hate any of them.

Who surprised me was my auntie. She rushed out of the house, alarmed by what was occurring.

"She is your niece and that is her mate. Help her," my auntie begged.

Back under full control, I revisited every law I'd memorized. My uncle was Alpha, but he never took the time to truly read every passage written. But as Sentinel it was my duty to know which laws to enforce.

It was Dean who helped me remember. His smile was slight but easy for me to see. He wanted me to figure it out.

My eyes widened and I let out a breath before speaking quickly. I'd found my freedom to live another day.

"No human shall be struck, maimed, and or killed by such wolf for any reason, as it is written under wolf law, title 20.71." My uncle's incredulous gaze brought out the confidence needed. I sat tall on my knees, my hand holding Danni's. If she didn't shift in the next half hour, she'd be dead. I wouldn't allow that to happen.

I looked to my uncle and continued. "Should such a time be permitted that a wolf uses deadly force, not only must a human be fully cognitive of our existence but intent on causing bodily harm to one's mate or cub. For any other wolf outside that notation should capture and imprison until council has given permission to kill or set human free with harsh punishment."

The Alpha's head jerked as if I'd insulted him and he looked at Dean, the elder wolf for confirmation. One small nod was all it took.

"And before you try and tell me she is not my mate because we're two women, remember one of the wolves on the council has a mate of the same sex. So, if you deny me of my right to protect and prosecute my mate's attacker you also deny his and every other wolf's who loves the same sex." I wouldn't continue to defend my connection to anyone or pretend anymore.

Jenkins smiled, relief settling in his loose shoulders.

My auntie moved to my side. "Now that we have that issue cleared up, it's time—"

"Go inside. I have no need for your antics." My uncle dismissed his mate, and I wondered if he had ever loved her. Perhaps he had once until he'd been consumed by greed. His lust for power made it impossible to love anything.

But my auntie had shocked me a second time. "If you don't save this young innocent wolf, you'll be the first Alpha to have his mate leave."

That would make him look weak. If he couldn't keep his mate in line and at his side, how could he control his pack? His nostrils flared by her threat.

Eyes narrowed; my uncle growled. "Then leave!" He challenged. "Where would you go?" he taunted. "Your old pack no longer exists. No pack would take in another Alpha's mate. You'd be alone, something you've feared for years."

I lowered my head and noticed Danni's breathing was labored. We didn't have much time. Danni barely moved, only the slow rise and fall of her chest showing she was still alive. Her wolf couldn't rise to the surface, caged more tightly than she'd ever been. All I wanted was for Danni's pain to go away and to see her eyes look upon me. Have her fall into my scent and run at my side as wolves. Hunt and kill together. I hadn't kissed her or held her in my arms yet. My wolf wanted it all. I wanted it all. More than I wanted anything in my life. More than I wanted this pack.

"I'll leave," I said.

And there it was. His second hope alive in his eyes. He'd been waiting for me to say those words. I didn't care.

"No!" I heard Jenkins shudder out in disbelief.

"Quiet!" My uncle said, abruptly.

I straightened my spine, chin raised high. "Call my mate's wolf out and I will denounce myself to this pack for as long as you remain Alpha."

"And your mate must never come and try to claim this pack," he added.

I nodded. "We will not come and challenge you to the position of Alpha."

His smile widened. "You will leave the minute—"

"I must complete what I started," I explained before he finished his words. "Under pack law, once a Sentinel has begun an investigation, it is my duty to complete what has already been set in motion. I cannot betray that oath, even upon my untimely departure to this pack."

My uncle let those words twirl in his thoughts until he nodded.

"Be quick. It is agreed."

I nodded. "Now, save my mate!" I demanded. As of this moment, I was no longer his. All he needed was my words to seal my new fate. The pack had been his witness. I'd worry about Danni and my future later. I needed her wolf to come out.

"Tame her," he snarled.

Since Danni was not conscious, her wolf was easily forced by another Alpha to bend to his will, unlike before when she'd been in the cage I'd found her in. He tried to command her to shift.

My uncle didn't move toward us, shutting his eyes briefly as he touched a power within him that allowed him to force her shift. I still doubted he was a born Alpha, but I didn't care what or who he was if he did what was agreed upon.

In an eerie hateful tone, he uttered the words, "Shift!"

Nothing happened right away. For a second, I thought it hadn't worked. Maybe Danni was too far gone. The thought terrified me, and I hated feeling that way. The longer it took, the more my anxiety overwhelmed me. I squeezed Danni's hand as if trying to squeeze life back into her before it was too late.

Everyone stood watching me. Though most didn't want Danni around, there were condolences directed at me. No wolf should lose a mate. My uncle seemed to be the only one smiling on the inside. Bastard.

Danni's eyes didn't flutter open. Her chest barely moved, and her wolf was barely a whisper of a cry. Shock overtook my mind, and I sucked in a deep breath before shuddering air out from my lungs. Was this it? My happy ending?

It was Dean who spoke, rattling my brain with possibilities.

"Bite her!" He whispered.

His words made no sense to me, but my wolf understood immediately and didn't waste time. I called to my wolf, teeth elongated, and I pulled Danni's arm up, biting down hard. I waited for something to happen, half expecting Danni to finally stir. Impatience grew along with renewed fear when my wolf howled, calling for her mate. Danni's wolf was lost, but my wolf would find hers.

There. Hidden deep within the silhouette of Danni's restless soul. A wolf alone, curled tightly in a corner. Darkness and pain keeping her detained. My wolf found her, head lifting in confusion. Danni's wolf thought she'd never be found. But I did.

I pulled my mouth from Danni's arm, eyes shut as I whispered, "I claim you, as my mate. Now and forever." Tears swelled around my eyes, knowing there was no going back. Danni and I would have a long journey ahead but what mating bond was ever easy? Ours would certainly be unique. But there was no shame.

Danni's fingers tightened around mine and she groaned. When her eyes opened, they were a bright amber. Her wolf was in control. She moved so quickly, lifting from the ground only to leap into a shift, clothes shredding and falling to the floor.

I leaped back in shock. Her shift was fast, and everyone took a step back.

My uncle lifted his hand and then dropped it back. He was about to point at Danni but remembered she didn't like being pointed at. Smart man.

"Get her out of here," my uncle hollered.

Danni moved to my side, brushing her body along my thigh. I ran my fingers over her ear, assuring her we were safe. "What happened to the wolf we found? He should—"

Jenkins answered before I finished. "I took care of him."

He didn't need to say more. I trusted in whatever decision he made. We couldn't turn his body into the police or report the newly turned wolf's death, but we could give him a proper burial. Whoever he was in the past no longer mattered. It was too much of a risk to have a werewolf turned into the hands of human doctors that would run his DNA.

I glanced at everyone who was nearby. They were no longer my pack. Right now, I couldn't grieve them, but I knew eventually this moment would hit me hard. Giving Dean a nod of appreciation, I turned my back on everyone. As soon as we were out of eyesight, I'd shift and run freely with Danni.

"Don't forget. Once you swiftly get rid of the rogues trespassing, you are to leave my territory within 24 hours." My uncle wanted to make sure there was no confusion in my future.

I didn't bother stopping or acknowledging him and walked away with my mate at my side. A mate who was oblivious to what had transpired.

*

*Danni*

My wolf had run beside Karissa's, wild and free throughout the night, unable to shift back to human until break of dawn. There was something different in the way my wolf acted around Karissa's, a bond forming without my awareness. We'd ended up in Karissa's small and concealed backyard, still as wolves, falling asleep under the stars.

My eyes fluttered open to see the sun leaking through the bushy trees, rays of yellow and orange filling my vision. Birds chirped and a few squirrels scuttled by, keeping their distance, aware that we were more than human. The grass was prickly, soil firm and dry despite the brief rain in the middle of the night. The air was fresh, trees, flowerbeds, and the soil beneath, appeasing my wolf.

Karissa's soft breathing was the best music to my ears as she slept curled against me. At some point after shifting back, Karissa had closed the distance between us. Her head was pressed into my shoulder, breast against my own, with one of her legs draped between my legs. Her arm snaked across my waist possessively.

We were both naked and it wasn't something I was used to. Anytime I'd shifted in the past, I'd always be alone when I woke up. But I found myself comfortably naked in front of her, not self-conscious of my body. My life was not fortunate enough to worry about embarrassing moments.

The last thing I remembered last night was leaping over Karissa, saving her from a silver arrow. After that, my memory was foggy and questionable. My wolf had led most of the night, leaving me with only vague images of us hunting together. I liked being with Karissa. There was an energy inside her that grounded and excited me at the same time.

"Your heart's beating really fast," Karissa mumbled, groggily.

My brows arched and I wondered if she could tell what I'd been thinking. I tried to tell my heart to slow down but it seemed to only pound faster. It was unrealistic to believe a woman like Karissa would find me compelling. Some part of her had to pity me.

Doubt about our connection trickled into my head like a dark angel feeding me false leads. I was on the verge of self-sabotaging the connection I had if I let the fear and doubt linger.

Karissa's head lifted and she cupped my cheek, drawing me in. Her soft gray eyes held my brown ones. Tender and lovingly.

"Don't do that," she said.

Maybe she could read my thoughts.

"Are you a psychic too?" I asked, half-jokingly.

Karissa snorted and rolled her eyes. "No, silly. I just..." she hesitated to finish her words, tone dropping down a pitch. "I just...know."

Such simple words that conveyed so much. There was something Karissa wasn't telling me. But it didn't matter. I wanted to be around her no matter what and hoped it wouldn't just be a fantasy in my head.

"You are very important to me. I mean that." Karissa's feathery fingers grazed my cheek and tugged the small strands above my ear.

My stomach flipped, twisted, and fluttered at the way Karissa continued to look at me. I was being mesmerized and I didn't care if she sent me off a cliff. I'd still follow.

It suddenly became harder to breathe, in need of something more than soft affectionate touches to sate my lustful needs.

Karissa eyes dropped to my lips and my nipples tightened from anticipation. I was turned young and hadn't had any opportunity to explore and feel intimacy. I'd never been aroused before, and it felt painfully good. A throbbing between my legs made itself known and I didn't know what to do with these new feelings.

"Thank you for saving me," she whispered.

I blushed, not used to hearing words like thank you.

"I would never let anything happen to you." I wanted Karissa safe from everyone.

Karissa smiled cheekily. "Who's giving out promises now?"

I surprised myself, realizing I'd given her a promise and meant it. Most of my life I'd known 'promise' to be a meaningless word but saying it now, I finally saw its value. I'd grown to hate that word over the years but suddenly I found the depth of its meaning and sincerity. Promises were kept by those who cared about you. And I cared about Karissa more than I knew how to explain.

"Maybe you're rubbing off on me," I joked, nervous and shy, trying to not be obvious about my feelings for her.

I was painfully reminded that we were both naked when Karissa's nipples hardened against my flesh. These strange foreign feelings should have scared me, but it was Karissa. I was nervous but not scared. Okay, maybe a little but only fearing she didn't feel the same. I tried to distract myself. What if I wasn't ready for whatever this was? What if I was seeing what I wanted to see? What if I was too much of a wolf? Who wanted to be with something savage like me? I needed to get Karissa out of my head before I said something foolish.

Moving the conversation along, I asked, "What happened—"

Karissa pressed her finger against my lips. "Shush." Sliding forward, her head hovered over mine, breathless with need in her burning gold eyes.

This was comfortable. She fit perfectly in my arms. With the way she stared at me, I wondered if I wasn't the only feeling something.

Then her finger grazed slowly and intimately over my bottom lip, watchful like a wolf surveying her meal. The way her eyes lingered on my lips, I was sure she'd do what I'd been longing for. Would it be soft and brief or hard and lustful? I wanted to find out.

And just as Karissa moved in, as if to kiss me, a man's voice echoed along the side of the house. I'd been swept away by Karissa's essence; I hadn't smelled him coming. Instinctively, I flipped Karissa onto her back, protective and guarded as the familiar man opened the six-foot gate where he walked from the front of the house.

It was Karissa's brother, Tanner. When he noticed us, Tanner quickly averted his head, grunted his disapproval, and didn't bother turning around. He didn't trust me enough to turn his back to me, and I couldn't blame him. My wolf didn't want him near Karissa, after he'd grabbed her the first time we met. I was still in control, but my wolf was ready to lead if trouble came knocking. The fact that he was Karissa's brother meant nothing to me. I'd been sold to Hansel by my own father and Karissa's uncle wanted her dead. Being of blood relation held no merit in my wolf's eyes, nor my human mind. I knew eventually I'd have to work on blending in with my wolf and ultimately being the one in control, but I hadn't been free from Hansel for more than a few days. It would take time if I was fortunate to stay out of his grasp long enough.

Karissa whispered my name and I eventually glanced down at her beneath me. I hadn't known when she had pressed her hand against my cheek.

"Danni." She said my name a bit louder, and my wolf was finally ready to listen.

Tanner stayed within my sight as I briefly glanced down at Karissa, who was smiling up at me.

"He won't hurt me." She seemed sure but I wasn't.

I let out a slow, begrudging breath. I trusted Karissa and her judgement, but my wolf was not hearing it.

Karissa's soft lips brushed my chin in a tantalizing kiss and my wolf gave in, ready to roll on her back and give her belly. That's all it took to calm my wolf. Those soft lips. I wanted to feel them again.

"Trust me, my rogue wolf!" She grinned when my wolf peeked out.

Slowly, I moved off, helping Karissa to her feet as we stood together. Here we were, naked in the backyard, thankfully secure enough to not have nosy people peek over, with her brother standing at a safe distance. He looked like he wanted to escape but was too determined to come and say what he needed. I bet he didn't expect to see us in that position, as if Karissa's actions the past few days had been out of character.

"Um..." Karissa seemed at a loss for words until she came up with something to say. "I should go grab us some clothes." She didn't give it a second thought, trusting my wolf would stay at bay. "I'll be right back." She squeezed my arm in reassurance. "And please, play nice." She looked to her brother before running off.

I wanted to ask why we couldn't go inside the house, but my wolf had given me the answer. Being in a closed space with Tanner would be unsettling and trigger a murderous outburst. And my wolf wouldn't think twice. I smiled, trying to do what Karissa wanted. Play nice.

# Chapter Twelve

*Karissa*

I quickly dressed and then foraged through the dresser in the room Danni was staying in to find her something to wear.

Flustered, heat swarmed my body. Incapable of shoving my emotions to the back of my mind, I replayed the private moment we had shared before my brother interrupted us. I'd been close to kissing Danni and now that was all I could think about. Warmth reddened my cheeks and I found myself smiling.

There had never been a time before Danni where I daydreamed and longed for someone to make me feel the way she did. If this was a dream, I had no intentions of waking up. As if a light switch had turned on, accepting Danni as a mate was the force to finally let myself live in the moment.

"Get a grip," I mumbled to myself.

There was no positive energy between Danni and my brother. Not after she'd knocked him on his ass, ready to rip his throat out. His intrusion would not be forgotten in Danni's eyes, nor my own since he'd interrupted a private moment.

My brother wasn't here for a random visit, so I tried taking that into consideration. I'd given my uncle what he'd been wanting for years, and my brother wasn't pleased by my choice. Denouncing myself from the pack wasn't as difficult as I'd thought it would be. But as much as my brother wanted me close, part of him had to be relieved I'd be leaving, no longer feeling a strain of loyalty between my uncle and me.

Once I found a pair of sweats and a shirt, I wasted no time heading back to my mate and brother.

My mate. Who would've thought I'd ever say that? Danni was protective of me. It would be a mistake to bring both of them within the same walls. It would make Danni's wolf feel as if the walls were closing in on her, along with unfriendly wolf barricades inside as well.

I took in my home and sighed. Soon, it would no longer be mine. I'd have to pack my things and move out of my uncle's territory. The only home I'd known.

I found Danni standing in the same spot, my brother pacing at a safe distance. Stepping through the sliding door, I walked outside toward Danni, handing her the clothes.

She dressed, never stripping her gaze from my brother. Her wolf flickered in and out of her eyes and I found it best to linger at her side. Maybe touch would keep her wolf at bay. I reached in, sliding my fingers between hers and squeezed.

"Now's not the best—"

My brother cut me off, fist balled, with an expression that I was sure many feared. Not me and certainly not Danni.

"You have certainly dug yourself into a fucking hole that I can no longer dig you out of." He snarled in between words as if it was hard for him to breathe. His neck strained, fighting back his wolf.

"I never asked you to dig me out of anything." I hadn't yet shared with Danni the events that had transpired at pack home. It wasn't something I wanted to discuss in front of my brother. "How about you call the next time you want to just show up?" I advised.

His frown deepened, fixing his gaze onto Danni before growling.

Domina Alexandra

"You are sacrificing yourself for nothing." His words were directed toward Danni, who could grasp that she was out of the loop.

It wasn't Danni that moved toward my brother, it was me. He didn't expect me to do anything, so when my palm slammed into his chest sending him flying backward several feet into my flowerbed, he groaned, looking dumbstruck. Slowly, he crawled to his knees, standing up. Tanner brushed dirt from his pants and then hands, giving me a blank stare.

"Maybe it is for the best that you leave. The sooner the better," he said.

He didn't say anything else. Just turned and left.

I stood there, filled with adrenaline and unable to say anything. He'd insulted my mate and I couldn't stand for it. He knew better and didn't care. I knew my brother. The only reason he had tried to protect me this long was for my parents and the obligation they had enforced in his mind since my birth.

There was never a moment I saw in my brothers eyes a personal desire to protect me, when all I wanted was his love. But he'd lived a long time and lost two of his children. What love he had was gone with them and my parents.

"What was he talking about?" Danni asked.

I sighed, not ready for this conversation. Talking about it meant I had to acknowledge it. I'd spent nearly a century with my pack, and I was leaving it. Something I never wanted but as long as my uncle was Alpha, me leaving was inevitable. There was no regret in my decision.

So instead of being sad about it, I faced Danni, confident and ready to answer her questions.

"I have ended my tie to the pack."

Danni's eyes widened, bewildered. Letting my words sink in, Danni pressed her fingers into the corners of her forehead, brows kneading together.

"I thought you said he couldn't kick you out without just cause."

I shared everything that had transpired last night, telling her about what I'd done after finding out she'd been shot with the arrow, ultimately killing one of the humans.

When I was done, Danni shifted her head, staring up at the sky, impassively.

I couldn't tell what she was thinking and that made me nervous.

"I'll be fine." Maybe I was fooling myself, but I didn't want Danni doing anything rash.

Danni frown deepened. "You will go to your pack and plead with him to take you back."

"I can't do that."

"Yes, you can!" she snapped. Danni turned from me, taking this harder than I had expected. "I will leave because I refuse to stand by and be the cause of you losing your pack."

I shook my head. Her threat of leaving panicked my wolf.

"I'm not going back, Danni. And I wouldn't if I could." Even if I found myself weak enough to go back and grovel at his feet, my uncle wouldn't take me back. The decision was final.

When she faced me again, tears fell down her cheeks and she was unable to meet my eyes.

"You shared stories about your pack. They're family. Don't let all that go because of me. I'm not who you think I am."

Why was she taking this so hard? There had to be more. It hurt losing the pack but if I was honest with myself, I hadn't felt a part of this pack in years. I smiled and closed the distance between us.

"I told myself I was staying to protect what my mom had built. But the truth is, I couldn't let go of the past." As I said the words, I realized how true they were.

There were so many memories here and the thought of leaving it all behind terrified me. But it hurt more being rejected by half of the pack due to my uncle purposely working to isolate me from them all.

"You are the one that matters to me now. I'm happy with my decision."

Danni shuddered and averted her gaze to the ground. Her body trembled, some deeply rooted emotion coming to the surface. It wasn't anger. No, I'd seen that. This was different. Pain. Regret. Self-loathing.

"I've done things." I could barely make out her words from her broken tone.

"We all have."

Danni's head shook. "No," she whispered. She was fidgety, standing hunched and awkward. "I've...killed innocent people." Danni's eyes found mine, so much shame, regret, and pain.

Her words took a few heartbeats for me to process. I craned my neck, my turn to stare up at the sky. I knew there was more to her story. No witch wolf had worked so hard to keep control of her only to keep her in fighting pits. He'd groomed Danni to be his wolf assassin. And one day, her sins would catch up with her and that was something I had to accept if this was going to work. When I looked back at Danni, she stood guarded and ready to run.

Despite what she had told me, despite knowing her only a few days, I knew her. Saw through her shields, finding the heart beating within her chest.

"You were taken as a child. Sold by your father." I inhaled sharply and let it out slowly, trying to keep tears at bay. I hated how her life as a werewolf had come to be, but I couldn't change that and needed to let go. And Danni needed to more than anyone. She couldn't keep punishing herself. "You were forced into a world that can be very dark and scary. I couldn't imagine being in your shoes. Being brought in that way. Never learning to control your wolf. Seeing it as a beast. Being told and I'm sure forced to kill for him. That's why you stayed so long." It was a statement that rocked Danni's demeanor.

"You wanted to punish yourself for being his wolf assassin. And he made you think it was all you had to offer the world," I continued. I took another step and this time played with the ends of her hair. "You are stronger than him. He does not own you. And you need to forgive yourself. So, you can forget leaving me and going back to that piece of shit because I'm not going anywhere but with you."

For the longest time, Danni and I stared at each other in comfortable silence until she collapsed into my arms. She held me tightly, face tucked into the curve of my neck, crying. I held her firmly, brushing my hands over her back in circular motions.

We stood like this for some time. I wanted to be there every step of the way. Wipe her tears when she cried. Keep her safe in my arms.

When Danni finally pulled away, I wiped some of her tears as well as mine and smiled. "Now let's go hunt us a witch wolf."

\*

It had taken most of the day to reach out to my sources. I had created my own network of associates, separate from the pack, several years back once I knew I wouldn't gain any assistance. My uncle had never wanted me as a Sentinel and without a pack at my side, there was a limit to what I could do. The risk of being killed increased when I investigated rogues with no backup.

Night was surfacing and soon all supernaturals would be out prowling. Since my car had been hit with several arrows and a dead wolf had bled out inside, we'd have to use the motorcycle I kept tucked away in the garage.

"I've missed you." I was having personal time with my motorcycle. I removed the covering and ran my finger over the slick surface. It was painted black and purple with silver sparkling rims.

Danni stared, not able to conceal a smile. "Purple, huh?"

I rolled my eyes, swung my leg across and took a seat.

"Purple happens to be my favorite color."

"It suits you," Danni grinned.

"Smart ass," I said. "Climb on."

Danni slid on behind me, curling her arms around my waist. She felt good, her body warming mine. As if she was trying to arouse me, though I knew she was clueless, Danni brushed her nose along the nape of my neck, breathing in my scent. I exhaled, nearly letting out a whimper. My skin flushed, goosebumps rising down my spine.

"Are you okay?" Danni spoke softly in my ear.

What she was doing was making things worse. I wanted her and timing was against us. What I'd do to kiss her now. I readjusted her hands around my waist and let out a quiet but shaky breath.

"I'm fine."

Not giving her a chance to ask me another question, I fired up my motorcycle and sped out onto the road, hopefully headed to some answers.

We parked on the border of pack territory, meeting up with my contact. I armed myself with a short blade, several throwing knives, and a gun with wooden bullets. We didn't have many vampires in our part of town but occasionally the undead liked to come and cause trouble.

We pulled into a park, vast and spacious, a pond glistening below the nearly full moon. We found a trail and walked down its path, into the woodsy area. The trail was condensed, gloomy trees hovering over both ends, making the path feel claustrophobic. It was dark, no humans around to worry about if trouble announced itself.

"You trust this person?" Danni leaned against a tree, arms crossed over her chest, when we stopped at our meeting spot. She wasn't trusting of anyone except me and needed to know we were not about to walk into a trap.

"No," I answered. "He's a rouge and a sketchy one. But no matter what happens tonight, he will bring us some answers."

From a distance, I heard him approaching and stood at the center of the trail. He noticed me and grinned widely; arms stretched out in an enthusiastic greeting.

"My favorite Sentinel. Shit, you look..." His mouth clamped shut when he noticed Danni move to my side.

I snorted, enjoying his discomfort since he was about to compliment me with his pervy looming eyes. He lacked tack and I tolerated his wandering gaze if he gave me the intel I asked for. But with Danni here, he'd be foolish to say anything or look at me inappropriately.

"Oh, hello," he said. He didn't bother offering a handshake, opting to slide them in his front jean pockets instead.

Danni took a step forward, eyes squinting with a look of recognition. Her lip curled with anger and accusation.

"I know you!" She spoke, adamantly.

"Oh," he looked to me for assistance. "I don't forget faces. You gotta be mistaken."

"I'm not." Danni looked ready to tear his arms off. "You go by Pete."

His eyes widened.

"How do you know him?" I asked.

"He was there the night we met. He works under Johnson," Danni explained.

Johnson was a well-known werewolf who moved all over California running illegal wolf fighting pits. I'd seen him there and he'd ran off before I had the chance to reach him.

Pete was young for a werewolf and a bit naïve, but he wasn't a high-ranking criminal. He took on a lot of odd jobs for rogue wolves because he was a rogue himself. It wasn't easy trying to support yourself without knowing the right people. And sometimes the wrong ones.

"Okay, yeah, I was there but that doesn't mean I know you." Pete stood defensive not sure what Danni might do next.

Danni explained further and when she was done, Pete's expression changed to excitement.

"Oh, shit. That was you in the cage." Exhilarated, Pete's smile widened like he'd been standing in front of a celebrity. "I should have known you were a werewolf. The way you fought. Shit, Johnson kept saying he wanted you after Sentinel here busted the party."

I rolled my eyes. "I was doing my job."

"Right," Pete said casually, not giving me any attention. He seemed too focused on Danni.

"He called you Hansel's wolf assassin. Rambled on about how your master—"

His words jolted my wolf awake and I snarled.

"Don't ever repeat those words again," I warned. In the corner of my eye, I saw Danni lower her head in shame. I reached over, grabbing her hand.

Pete noticed my movement and eyes widened. "My bad. I didn't realize—"

"Let's just move on to why I called," I interrupted.

"Right." Pete nodded. "When you asked about Hansel, naturally I went to the only person who knew him personally."

"Johnson," Danni muttered.

Pete nodded. "Seems those two have old beef. Anyways." Pete was naturally eccentric and a bit dramatic on normal days but tonight, he seemed to have taken a double dose of adrenaline since realizing who Danni was. His foot tapped vigorously, and he smiled awkwardly every time he made eye contact. "I didn't know she was a werewolf," Pete repeated.

Something was off. I sniffed the cool air and almost missed the stench of betrayal walking our way. "You've never betrayed me before."

143

Danni's head swerved in every direction, searching for the werewolves headed our way.

"I swear I thought he was after Hansel's prized wolf to claim. If I'd known she was a werewolf and you two bonded, I would have never told him about this meeting." Pete seemed more afraid of my disappointment than the wolves coming our way.

Truth was, I shouldn't have been surprised. Rogue wolves weren't loyal to anyone, and he was young. It was extremely dangerous being a lone wolf and I should not have expected him to be the perfect ally.

"It's okay. You should go," I suggested.

Danni frowned.

I reached out and squeezed her arm. "He no longer matters." I nodded up ahead at six rogue wolves headed our way. Johnson was leading. It was too late to run. They would only catch up.

No. It was better to face them now. By the stoic look in Danni's eyes, she wasn't willing to run either.

Johnson ambled, in no rush to reach us. His smug features expanded when he twisted his gaze to Danni, recognizing her right away. The five other wolves hid between the trees, stretched out, and caging us.

Lips pursed, as if he already had possession of Danni, he combed his thin fingers through his long beard.

"I always wondered what you looked like behind those wolf eyes." Johnson kept his interest on Danni, not concerned with my presence.

Danni wasn't normally this quiet for so long and I knew she was struggling to maintain leadership over her wolf. Her spine stiffened and her jaw popped on the verge of a shift.

"It's not too late to turn away," she snarled, through clenched teeth.

Johnson laughed, pressed his hand against his chest and shook his head in disagreement.

"You know I can't do that."

I narrowed my eyes along the trees to my right, sensing a wolf moving closer. He had to be fifteen feet from me. He smelled familiar and I knew he'd be the first one to pounce if things turned ugly.

"How about you at least entertain us by answering a few questions." I decided to try to get something out of him since he was here.

"I heard you are no longer a part of a pack. Fair game. There are a lot of weres looking to settle a score." Johnson smirked. "One here now."

I shrugged. "I might be a rogue now, but I'm not young nor naïve."

Johnson's voice rose in a commanding tone. "Come willingly or I kill your mate and take you anyway."

My eyes widened at his blunt demand. Danni didn't move or speak. I wondered if she was aware of anything. Her eyes seemed distant. Johnson called her my mate, something I had yet to explained, unsure of how to tell her.

"Does Hansel know you're trying to take Danni for yourself?" I asked, curiously.

Johnson snorted. "If he doesn't, he's an idiot. Who wouldn't want the wolf assassin? You have no idea who she is, do you?"

"Whoever she was, doesn't change—"

"No, now, Sentinel. Do not get ahead of yourself just because she makes you feel warm inside." Johnson straightened his spine, and I knew he was growing impatient with this conversation. "I doubt she even knows.

Hansel messed up her mind. What she thinks, might not be what is true." His furtive grin annoyed the shit out of me.

I knew he was right. Hansel was a witch wolf and could have spelled her mind into believing whatever he wanted. Being held captive for several years, who knew all he'd done to her and tricks he had hidden behind his secrets?

There was no point in trying to figure that out now. Even if Johnson had all the answers, which I doubted, he wouldn't have shared.

"My last act as Sentinel for this territory is to make sure no illegal fighting pits return and that Hansel is either handed to the council or killed," I announced. "Now, you can either assist or let's get on with this fight so we can be on our way."

Johnson didn't seem like the kind of guy who liked to be dismissed. His eyes narrowed and then looked off toward the trees. He was getting ready to signal his sidekicks.

"I will kill every wolf here and save you for last." Danni finally spoke, sheer power emanating out of her like a bomb ready to explode. Neck strained, muscles tight, her teeth elongated, capable of tearing through flesh.

"Still angry about that wolf I caged beside you, huh?" Johnson laughed.

"And all the other wolves you sent to their deaths," Danni stated. "But mostly, because my wolf does not like you." If looks could kill, Danni's would.

By Johnson's hesitant response, he was afraid. He took a step back and the wolves around us took several steps closer. Johnson wasn't a fighter. He'd run and we'd have to chase.

It would be easier fighting them in our current state, confident we could beat them. Since Danni hadn't shifted yet, she was on the same page.

The werewolf I'd sensed from the beginning leaped out, teeth and claws ready to tear into me. I pulled out my short blade, moving fast, and didn't hold back as I dodged then plunged my blade into his neck. He yelped, trying to reach me from his side, swiping his thick claws, desperate to win. I yanked the silver blade out, slammed him against the hard soil and slid the blade into his heart. He had no time to react, dying before his tail hit the ground.

I turned to see Danni fighting off two shifted wolves. She was composed and merciless, partially shifted claws shredding them apart, piece by piece. I'd seen Danni fight only once as her black wolf. She was fast, strong, and relentless. The same was true now in her human form. She killed one and another took its place.

I watched as one rushed Danni's backside, intent on baring his teeth into her flesh. I pulled out a throwing knife, released it swiftly from my fingers as it buried into the wolf's back. The wolf tumbled to the ground, paralyzed by the blade in its spine. I ran swiftly, catching one of the wolves fighting Danni and curling my arm around his neck, crushing it until I heard a pop. Neck broken, the wolf dropped to the ground, unconscious. It would eventually recover, along with the second wolf I fought, once the blade was out of its spine.

Danni was down to the last wolf who'd been the strongest of everyone. She seemed to match it in speed and strength. For every strike Danni connected, the wolf matched. But there was something fierce about Danni that made her stand out and inevitably overpower the wolf. She had grit and the unwillingness to lose. Every muscle in

Danni's body worked to win, dodging, and striking without hesitation.

Impatient, the wolf moved out of reach, canines exposed and snarled. The wolf hunched back on her hind legs and then leaped forward in a sprint. As the wolf reached her, I expected Danni to get out of the way, but instead she stood her ground and caught the wolf by the snout, clamping its mouth shut.

Danni flung the wolf high in the air and slammed it to the ground, pinning it in place. The wolf fought and resisted for several seconds, snarling and writhing underneath. But there was something about Danni's strength and preeminence that made the wolf suddenly tremble as if its worst fears were about to come true. Danni hunched over the wolf's neck, both hands flat on the soil. I'd never seen someone in human form dominate a shifted wolf, animalistically, without the need to shift.

The wolf's tail tucked between her legs, and she whined before shifting, the change fast. I watched in admiration and shock as the woman curled to her side in the fetal position, never looking up once. Her long dark hair was matted to her skin, damp from exhaustion.

Danni bear-crawled off the woman, spine straightening, and accessed the woman. She'd barely broken a sweat fighting the rogues, no trace of injury, the cuts over her skin already healed.

I stepped beside Danni as the woman crawled to her knees, awaiting her punishment. I brushed my hand over Danni's arm, and she looked up to me, shocking me with a smile. It was so innocent and pure, as if she'd found something within herself that she hadn't known existed.

"I've never..." her smile widened, and she shocked me even further pulling me into an embrace, arms tight round me. She took in a long breath, capturing my scent as she always did and didn't let me go right away.

Never mind the werewolves, dead, unconscious, kneeling beside us. They weren't going anywhere, and their fight was over.

I wouldn't pull away, needing this hug from her more than I realized. Touch was everything to a werewolf. But when it came from a mate, it held a deeper longing I'd never thought I'd feel or accept. How could I deny this for one second?

When we parted my wolf whined, ready to reach in for more. I needed to relax and smiled, promising my wolf more later. Not only was Danni my mate but, somehow, without me realizing Danni had become my wolf's Alpha. Danni had a long way to go before she could take on that position, but it didn't stop my wolf from claiming her as Alpha now. It was inside Danni, strong and willing to lead. But healing from the years of abuse and getting used to a human mind would take time for her to be ready. Besides, there was a lot more responsibility as an Alpha that Danni had to learn. And there was also the werewolf council who'd have to recognize Danni as a werewolf and Alpha. It seemed that since they were under Hansel's control, he'd managed to hide her from them.

"I've never fought for me before. Let alone someone..." Danni's words lingered at the tip of her tongue. She scratched the back of her head and smiled awkwardly.

I grinned, arching my brows in suspense. "Someone..."

The look on Danni's face was adorable.

"Someone...I care for a lot."

I tried to hide the giddiness boiling inside and I could hear my wolf purr. Gosh, I was being pathetic as if she'd said the *'L'* word.

"I care about you a lot too!" I admitted and blushed. I couldn't say more, not ready to dive into those deeper feelings yet, but I wanted to give her something back.

"Good," she whispered. "I'd hate to be the only one."

I smiled and turned my eyes toward the woman still sitting on her knees below us. She hadn't moved, probably fearing that Danni would punish her if she did. We needed to get back on the issue at hand.

"Johnson's long gone."

Danni shrugged. "He has always been wise about obscuring his scent. But fear is an aroma no one can hide. I can track him." Danni then nodded to the woman kneeling. "I didn't kill her for a reason. She is Johnson's granddaughter. I have seen her several times."

And Johnson would want her back. I smiled.

"You're amazing." I pulled out my phone and called Jenkins. I might not be a part of the pack, but I was finishing a job for them, and this was on pack territory no matter how close to the border we were. He'd come with a cleanup crew. As for the werewolves still alive, they'd be taken into custody for breaking werewolf laws except for the granddaughter. I'd use her as leverage to persuade Johnson to leave this territory for good and help us track Hansel.

"What's your name?" Danni asked the woman.

The woman didn't look up right away. She was too worried about Danni reacting.

"Answer!" Danni commanded.

The woman head lifted enough to show her soft Spanish features, brown round eyes and full lips. She looked barely 20, with a narrow face and petite build. She was naked but didn't bother hiding herself. Werewolves weren't known to be prudish since shifting around others was normal from birth. Only turned wolves initially struggled, having lived with human society's views in their minds for years.

"Rosita," she whispered.

"You know why I haven't killed you?" Danni crouched down, getting a better view of the woman.

The woman nodded her head. "Because you want to use mc to get to my grandfather," she said begrudgingly.

Danni huffed and reached toward the woman, lifting her gaze to meet hers for a moment.

"No!" she said.

The woman stared up, confused.

"Yes, I did not kill you because of who you are," Danni continued. "But it's not to use you."

It was my turn to stare in confusion. I stood patiently and quietly, awaiting her explanation.

"I can find your grandfather without you. And the truth is...if he cared for your wellbeing, you wouldn't be here, let alone by yourself." Danni made a great point. "I watched how he treated you on several occasions. I know what it's like to be treated like trash. I saved you, mostly because you didn't deserve to die."

Rosita's eyes widened. At that moment, I could see they both had a lot in common. They had lived without love for too long. Tears fell from the woman's eyes and soaked her face. Danni stood and offered a hand. Rosita took it.

I tilted my head and listened as Jenkins and four others made their way here.

"He will want her back," Danni said. "Once he knows she's alive. He can't help it. It will be about possession, not love."

I agreed.

"Do you want to go back?" I asked Rosita. We couldn't keep her if she wanted to leave and there were rules to follow.

Rosita sighed, defeat reforming in her eyes.

"No, but I have no choice. He has my two little brothers."

Danni's face hardened but she said nothing right away.

"I will give you my phone number. Memorize it. And when the day comes you are ready to leave with your brothers, call." I gave her my number and she recited it until she was comfortable that she remembered.

She looked to me and then Danni before nodding.

"Thank you."

We watched her leave, running through the bushes in the opposite direction of where Jenkins and the others were coming from. Being that I was about to lose my home and was now without a pack, I didn't know what made me think I could help her, but I wouldn't have been able to sleep at night without offering. By the calm beating in Danni's chest, it eased her as well that Rosita now had an option.

"What do we tell them?" Danni asked.

"We tell them the truth. Only way we keep my uncle out of our face a while longer. But leave Rosita out."

Danni whispered her agreement as Jenkins approached.

I tried not to show sadness when my eyes locked with Jenkins'. He'd been my best friend and despite not wanting to feel it, something had changed between us. Something that was uncontrollable, and I wasn't sure if we'd ever recover. So instead of welcoming him with a smile, I nodded and got straight to business.

# Chapter Thirteen

*Danni*

It had taken longer than intended for Jenkins to retrieve the werewolves and ask his invasive questions. But since Karissa's departure from a pack, it was evident she was treated differently with no privileges or leverage to getting her way.

I had no clue what a pack was supposed to look or feel like, but I knew Karissa's relationship with the pack hadn't been healthy. Her connection with Jenkins seemed sincere, but now there was a strain as if one decision was the knife cutting into their bond.

Karissa tried not to show the hurt in her eyes, but I saw it. When it was all over, the awkward stare between Jenkins and her lingered. Neither could get out of their own emotional barricades.

"Your uncle and your Alpha should not be the one who defines your bond." I looked to both, wishing they'd move past their hesitation and fears. "Don't let him define your relationship." I walked away, giving them a chance to speak in private.

I waited, leaning against a tree, lost in my thoughts. The evening was calm despite how it started, but it was far from over. I wasn't ready to call it a night and had every intention of seeing Johnson again.

Someone I didn't recognize inched their way in my direction, catching my attention. Her eyes were hesitant but hardened with pain and resentment. Somehow, I'd been the cause of her grief without knowing her name.

I huffed, crossing my arms in annoyance. "Say it, already!"

Her green eyes narrowed and for a second I thought she might try something, but she kept her feet grounded. I could tell she was around the same age as Karissa in all her wolf years and late twenties in her features. Freckles highlighted her cheeks and her nose squinted from a deep-set frown. She looked more handsome than pretty with chin–length blonde hair placed in a bun.

"Karissa meant a lot to many in our pack and because of you, she'll never be happy again."

My brows arched. "The impression I got was that no one stood up for her when your beloved Alpha gave her a choice to make." I was far from the strongest and had a lot of demons, but not once did anyone in Karissa's pack intimidate me. Over the past few days, my anxiety and trepidation about where I belonged and who I belonged to had changed drastically. I knew my ultimate test would be when I faced Hansel again, but I couldn't worry about that now.

Having Karissa by my side, I was more worried about her future than mine and that's what fueled me to stay strong. Her happiness and safety mattered above all else.

So, facing this woman had nothing to do with her offending me and everything to do with her not being a true friend and pack member for Karissa when she needed it the most. And I would never have her beg them on my behalf again.

"I might be someone new in her life, but happiness in your pack seems like a far stretched truth. Perhaps you are angry because the one person in the pack who made you happy was her, and now she's gone. That is for you to figure out for yourself."

The woman only stared with grueling eyes. By her reaction, she knew I was right. After a few seconds more, she turned and stormed away.

Karissa walked up a minute later and reached in for a hug.

"Thank you," she whispered.

I smiled, taking in a long breath. "Everything okay?" I didn't want to pry, so I opted for hopeful progress in her conversation with Jenkins.

Karissa nodded. "It will be." She looked toward her old pack and watched as they left with the werewolves over their shoulders. She tried not to show her sadness, but I knew. "I noticed Monica talking to you. Didn't seem too friendly."

I hadn't known the woman's name. "According to her, I ruined your life."

Karissa snorted.

"Hey, I know you weren't happy in the pack, but I didn't make things easier for you." I'd seen the disdain in her uncle's eyes the moment I entered the picture. Whatever dislike he'd been holding in for Karissa came out full speed when he noticed our connection. A connection I still didn't understand but everyone around me seemed to get.

"Yes, you sped things along but only for the good. I should have left long ago. But then again, I wouldn't have been here to meet you." Karissa leaned forward and pressed our foreheads together. "I need you in my life, so don't get any ideas. I'm not going back to that pack, no matter what happens," she whispered.

I found myself reaching in and pressing my hands to her waist. Everything inside me burned, wanting to tug her close and kiss her until our lungs were on the verge of explosion from lack of air. My wolf clawed inside to get closer and mark her. There was a need I was new to but couldn't bring myself to live without.

I let out a shaky breath and closed my eyes, trying to regain some composure.

"If we don't go now, we'll miss our chance at finding Johnson's scent."

Karissa groaned, and not from pain. She'd been feeling something too. When our eyes met, her gaze dipped to my lips and she groaned again, shaking her arms as if trying to shake off something that was more felt than seen.

"Okay. The sooner the better."

I smiled. "Sooner!" We didn't need to say any more and raced to her motorcycle.

*

I didn't need to shift to find Johnson; my human nose was very capable. I climbed off the motorcycle and twirled around, taking in the area. It took us an hour to arrive in a secluded truck stop in French Camp, Stockton.

"Is he that dumb?" Karissa parked a block away from the truck stop.

We couldn't see anything; trucks were placed strategically at every corner so no prying eyes could take notice to what was occurring. There were a lot of werewolves and humans gathered at the truck stop.

"It's quite ingenious for Johnson, at least." I walked to the edge of the sidewalk, vehicles flying past, ignoring the 45-mph speed limit. "We're on neutral ground. No pack owns this location." Karissa frowned and I explained, "I've fought here numerous times."

How many times had I gone into Karissa's territory and been close to seeing her? It had been my first time in the fighting pit inside her territory, but there were other reasons I'd been here in the past. Done things I wasn't proud of.

"I see." Karissa looked across the street where the truck stop resided a block down.

"He won't run. He has all the allies he needs. It would be risky walking in and expecting a fair fight." I knew what we needed to do and hoped Karissa would agree. "We have to go in as players," I said. Player was a term used in the fighting pit to signify who was bringing a wolf in to fight.

Karissa's head swerved, an argumentative glare pinning me in place.

"What?" She grabbed my arm and guided me away from the street. "Whatever you're thinking, no!"

I didn't expect us to agree on everything. My experience as a werewolf had given me a different perspective on life but I also appreciated Karissa's views and opinions. She believed there were always options. For me, I knew sometimes there was never another option.

I let myself sift through Karissa's intense need to keep me safe until I was left with the lingering truth.

"I am tired of waiting for the other shoe to drop. This is our chance to end things tonight."

"How?"

I smiled, weakly. "Letting me be the bait."

A Rogue's Redemption

"Danni…" Karissa didn't know what to say.

I knew my plan could backfire. Losing Karissa wasn't an option and trust needed to be tested between us.

"If I go in as a wolf ready to fight with you as my player, Johnson will not hesitate to use this to his advantage. And he won't out us because that could ruin his business since I've fought in his pits a half dozen times."

Karissa was about to argue but I continued. "Furthermore, I'm easily recognizable. And the veteran players know I belong to Hansel. Someone knows him and when he finds out I'm here, he won't be able to help himself and will challenge you to take me back. It would embarrass him."

The hardened frown crinkling Karissa's eyes softened, and I knew my words were sinking in.

"I hate this already."

"That's obvious."

Karissa narrowed her eyes at me and then smiled. "We have to make this play out in our favor. It is illegal in the eyes of werewolf law for a werewolf to fight in fighting pits. So, we can't go in as if I'm a player."

There was a lot I needed to learn about being a werewolf. Hansel never mentioned a werewolf council, let alone a set of laws. But that made sense, due to him breaking many of them, I'm sure.

"It can't be insinuated. Let Johnson do the talking." Karissa went over the plan and when she was through, she pulled out her phone and made a call.

I listened for a while but eventually drew my focus back to the truck stop. Hands brushed my shoulder. Karissa had my full attention.

"I want to make sure we are protected by council law. I know someone who works under the administration.

We're good. He'll send a couple agents within the council to come for the aftermath." Karissa took a long breath. "How do you want to do this?"

There wasn't much privacy around, but the antique store we were next to didn't have cameras and the lights were off. There was an archway with a spacious cove to conceal me from most passersby who weren't too curious. Fortunately, I shifted fast and could blend in beside Karissa when we were ready to head over.

"Wait." Karissa grabbed my hand before I could walk away. Her eyes softened on mine. "I don't want you to sacrifice yourself for me."

I opened my mouth to argue but she pressed her finger over my lips like this morning. Obediently, I closed my mouth and listened.

"I trust you explicitly. I need you to do the same. That means trusting that I'm capable of protecting myself and even you."

The argument failed at the tip of my tongue, and I nodded.

"I trust you." She was the only person I trusted, and we were mutually willing to put that to the test.

I moved to the antique shop, but Karissa didn't let go of her grip on my hand. Her eyes locked onto mine. She smiled and I blushed.

"Before we do this, I need you to know you aren't just someone I found in a cage."

Hearing that, I peered up at the sky, finally able to see the silver lining to my harsh life. I'd wondered for years: why me? I believed all my pain was worth it for this moment, knowing I'd be with Karissa for many years to come.

What I'd been feeling was authentic and reciprocated.

I'd heard what Johnson implied between Karissa and I and wanted her to be the one who told me.

"We're…" Karissa blushed, nipping her bottom lip.

"Mates," I finished. She'd been nervous to tell me, her voice in a higher pitch range than intended.

Karissa smiled and nodded. "Yes!"

"That word isn't lost on me but I'm sure there's more to it than I know. But I hope you know I want to explore that…with you."

"Good." Karissa's eyes dropped to my lips, and she sighed. "I don't want to rush this." She was breathing heavily, and I wasn't sure if she was talking more to me or herself.

I smiled. "Then we won't." As tempting as it was to lean in and kiss Karissa, there was a lot I needed to learn. How to accept and love a part of myself I thought was dark and monstrous. I feared what I was capable of and if I wasn't careful, I could hurt Karissa.

"Give me a second to shift." Unable to stop myself, I closed the distance between us and brushed my lips against her cheek.

I turned and headed under the archway. I removed my clothes and in one slow breath, shifted into my wolf. I shook my black fur, settling into my new shape. My wolf stretched out the front of my body, leaning back on my hind legs and letting out a loud yawn.

Having been in human form for a majority of the last few days, I'd missed being in my wolf's body. I knew it was out of comfort and safety reasons.

Karissa walked up to me, running her fingers through my fur, and smiled.

"You gained some weight."

My neck craned, not sure if that was a compliment. My wolf nipped Karissa's finger playfully and she laughed.

"It's a good thing," Karissa explained. "You were thin. You are starting to shape into the wolf you're supposed to be." She sighed and turned, facing the truck stop. "It's now or never."

I brushed my body against hers in agreement and then looked up, waiting for her to take the lead. As we approached, no one noticed us at first, too focused on the current fight. Tonight, the crowd was different than the last fight I'd been in, less organized and governed. Johnson had thrown this fight together last minute, knowing I'd find him. He'd have a better chance at living, surrounded by his associates. A couple truck headlights beamed in the direction of the parking spaces centered in the lot that had been converted into a fighting pit, highlighting the two wolves covered in blood and jagged cuts.

There was over fifty werewolves and humans, money in hand, betting on the spot for the wolf they believed would win. The stench of blood snapped my attention to the two wolves, savagely trying to kill each other. The two wolves mirrored blind rage and the need to survive.

The ambiance triggered memories of my first time being forced to fight. Confused and scared, wanting to wake up from my nightmare. But it had been real and one of the worst nights I ever faced. That night taught me, if I wanted to live, I needed to let go of my humanity and be the monster Hansel wanted me to be. That was how I kept fighting. From then on, I'd been known as the undomesticated wolf that killed unsparingly.

The fight ended with the red-haired wolf ripping into the other's neck.

I could sense Karissa's utter disgust and I wondered if that had been directed toward me. I'd been that red wolf, blood dripping from my fangs and wanting more. Karissa brushed her fingers behind my ears.

"Wariness leaks from your pores." Karissa drew my attention to her eyes and then nodded toward many cheering in celebration and collecting their bets. "I'm disgusted by them. Getting off on something so horrific and traumatizing to the wolves and werewolves like you, forced to fight. You didn't deserve this. I trust you," she continued, "but I can admit I do not want you to fight tonight and I'm afraid that's exactly what Johnson will want. I will do whatever I can to avoid that."

Karissa's passion in protecting me made me fear how far she might go.

I knew she meant it and wouldn't support me fighting unless every option was eliminated. But no matter how many times she planned to deny Johnson or a chance for me to fight, I knew that's exactly what I was going to do.

# Chapter Fourteen

*Karissa*

I wanted to protect Danni from all of this but was easily reminded this had already been Danni's world for a long time. There was no number of days that could go by without Danni forgetting what she'd been through. And I knew there would be hard days ahead until Danni could finally talk about her past without being swept up in a wave of heavy emotion.

"We've been expecting you." Johnson grinned and clapped his hands together as if celebrating. Four more werewolves stood closely behind him, guarding him, ready to attack if necessary. He knelt, several feet from Danni, rubbing the palms of his hands together. Then his eyes peeked up at me. "You decide to hand me my wolf?"

An audience was forming around us as a few noticed Danni's wolf. Casually, I watched for anyone pulling out their phone to make a call. Someone would call Hansel and when he came, I needed to be ready for whatever trick, magical deception, or persuasive speech Hansel might pull to get Danni back.

Danni had grown stronger in the passing days, but Hansel was her Achilles heels that would test her resistance. They shared a forceable bond that she succumbed to.

"I'm here so that she can cut ties with everyone and be free." There was no immediate reaction from Johnson, and I stepped forward, drawing his attention. "She doesn't belong with anyone," I muttered.

His eyes found mine briefly before glancing back to Danni, who was remarkably holding back her desire to rip through him.

Johnson's brow raised inquisitively.

"I wonder why no one can tell you are werewolf. I know Hansel had to use magic to conceal you but now...why is it?" His question was only loud enough for Danni and me to hear, confirming Danni's belief that he wouldn't want others to know. "Perhaps you have been more wolf, and for too long." He nodded and stood. "I will take the wolf. As for you, it was stupid to come here, out of your jurisdiction. Or do you not have a pack to lean on even as an ally anymore? I heard rumors of your strained relationship with that incompetent Alpha."

"Hey, we want to see her fight!" someone random called from the crowd gathering at a distance. They were talking about Danni. She'd built a fierce reputation and collected a lot of unwanted fans.

Johnson grinned, an idea forming in that small brain of his.

"A fight." He ran his fingers through his beard. "Hmm." He looked to the crowd and grinned, playing the host. "A fight!" he called out to the crowd this time, turning and giving them his attention.

A few cheered at the possibility.

I wanted to take Danni and get the hell away from here. I looked down at her, reminded of my promise to trust her, and grimaced. Danni had known this was coming and I'd been leaning on the possibility of another outcome, but an idea came to mind. One I knew could work.

165

"How about I fight in her place and when I win, you and anyone else are done bothering her?" I shouted loud enough for everyone to notice me. Some frowned my way, recognizing me for the few times I chased them out of my territory.

Johnson was about to brush off my request, but I continued, using the disdain some of the werewolves here had for me to my advantage.

"I know some of you want to fight me. Here's your chance. You set the rules."

Danni snarled in disapproval, and I took a step forward, willing her to do the same in trusting me and my abilities to survive. For once in her life, Danni would have someone fighting for her.

"It's not a fair fight, having a werewolf fight a bunch of mundane wolves," an older man hissed in disapproval.

I smirked and looked directly toward Johnson, whose expression was blank. If people found out Danni was a werewolf, it would be more than his reputation on the line. His life would be threatened for placing a werewolf in such confined conditions. Many didn't like me, but there were rules and caging another werewolf like a wild animal to be battered on a regular basis wasn't something they'd wish on any werewolf. It took a sadistic werewolf to treat another that way. One like Hansel and Johnson. Everyone here just came for the entertainment, however harsh that was.

"Of course. I see some old friends here. You both seem like you are interested in fighting me." Now I was antagonizing them. Two men stepped forward, one of them being the bouncer guarding the V.I.P section when I'd forced my way past to get to Danni. He didn't look pleased

166

seeing me here now and instinctively he reached for his chest, reliving my hand slamming against it, snapping his sternum in two. As for the second man, he'd been a drifter wolf that came in and out of my territory like a tornado, leaving a lot of pain and misery behind. His long black hair was pulled into a tight ponytail, his big forehead standing out more.

But then a third man came to view, one I didn't recognize by sight but by scent. His bushy brows knitted together into a unibrow, amber eyes piercing me with a vendetta to settle. He wasn't masculine or intimidating by size but instead lean and a few inches shorter than me. But the thirst in his eyes told me he wasn't someone to underestimate.

He pointed at me and as if it been directed at Danni, she lunged for him.

"Danni, no!" I called out but it was too late.

Danni leaped into the air and just as she reached him, she was halted by an unseeable force and twisted backwards, flipping, and then tumbled to the ground.

Everyone took several steps back, unsure what had happened.

But I knew. I could smell him before anyone else could and tried to hide my shock at how fast he'd arrived. I moved quickly to Danni, and she stood slowly, tail tucked between her legs. He was doing this. Using magic to force her into submission.

My shoulders stiffened and I snarled, glancing past Johnson at the figure approaching.

Hansel strode through the crowd and when he came to Johnson's side, he patted him on the shoulder and squeezed tightly. I watched Johnson conceal the pain, putting on a smile for the audience.

"I know you aren't about to fight my wolf without my consent," Hansel said to Johnson in an eerie tone.

Johnson breathed out slowly. "Of course not." Then his eyes fixed on me. "We were about to have a good old brawl between the Sentinel and a few werewolves here. I suspected someone would reach out to you."

"Right!" Hansel walked up to us, expecting me to take a step back so he could freely reach Danni's submissive body.

When I didn't move his eyes sunk into mine. I stared back, far from intimidated, my spine straight.

"She is no longer yours to abuse."

"You think so." Hansel blindly reached down and ran his fingers through her fur. Danni didn't move and, despite wanting to snatch his hand away, I held my composure.

"I can't stop you from running these illegal fights pits all over the country, but you will stop coming into my territory," I argued to Hansel and everyone else.

"Your...territory?" Hansel questioned; a grin plastered across his face.

"As Sentinel, it is my duty to complete a job even after I have resigned from a pack," I explained. "I found her when you left her in a cage at an illegal fighting pit. She is under my protection and custody. So, I advise you to back the hell up." The potency of my words was deafening enough to be felt.

Hansel had no interest in proving his dominance and dropped his eyes down to Danni, considering his options. He knew if he didn't back up, I'd tell everyone Danni was a werewolf he'd taken as a child. I wanted to use that as my weapon when I needed it most.

"Then I'll fight you," Hansel said before backing up.

My eyes widened.

He caught my shock and smiled devilishly.

"That was your plan before I interrupted, right?" He waved toward the men who'd been eager to fight me, dismissing them. "Never mind them. We have something bigger at stake. A fight to the death."

I tried not to show my shock. I stared down at Danni, who whined her disapproval and grimaced. Did she fear I would lose? I stared into her eyes and saw her concern. No! It was more than that. She feared he'd cheat, using his magic. Once Danni had told me about Hansel; she'd shared he lived by no rules but his own. He never fought his own battles. Yes, he'd cheat and do it unnoticeably.

But I had to do this. If only to prolong the significant players' stay here, long enough for the council's agents to arrive. Hansel would cheat but I'd be ready.

"I win, any bond you have over her is dissolved." I waited for his response and noticed his trepidation. "Do we have an agreement?"

After a fleeting heartbeat, Hansel nodded. He turned away and began walking to the center of the lot, where the two wolves finished their fight. He stripped off his jacket and shirt, tossing them to the ground.

I knelt beside Danni, running my fingers through her fur. We were at eye level as I whispered softly before kissing her snout.

"Trust me. My mother prepared me for nights like this. I will win."

Danni stared from me to Hansel warily, ready to shift and argue to take my place. But I knew her even if she didn't know herself. She wasn't ready to fight him. He'd come in hot with magic and she'd be taken by surprise, submitting out of instinct. There was just too many years of abuse and control between them. No one could get over that in a few months, let alone a few days.

"It's my turn to protect you," I said, standing.

Hansel was waiting for me, a path opening as people moved out my way.

"How do you want to do this? Wolf or human?" he asked.

I knew he was expecting me to say wolf because I would be able to dominate more as an experienced fighter. But I didn't know how his magic worked. As far as Danni knew, he was a born witch and wolf, a rarity that could make him unstoppable in either form if his magic assisted. By the intense glare he was putting my way, I knew he had unseen tricks up his sleeve in wolf form.

"Human." I muttered through gritted teeth. "And if we are still standing after five minutes, we shift."

"Rules to your liking?" Hansel asked Johnson who had been staring in amazement.

Johnson had his goons setting bets, and I was sure the total was much higher than it was supposed to be. This was still his gig, so final approval had to come from him. He pursed his lips, as if this had all been his idea and he was giving his final input.

"Let us tip the scale a bit."

"How so?" I scowled, not liking where this was going.

"I deem it unfair for some of my guys not to get in on the action. So, for every minute that passes, one can enter the fight." He let his teeth show when he smiled.

He was trying to get rid of me. Hansel and I would fight and then be shoved off balance, with one wolf after the next leaping in to attack. I knew it would give Hansel the chance to use his magic in significant ways since most of the werewolves had issues with me more than him. It was a smart tactic. No one would attack Hansel, and this was going to be a harsher fight than I realized. If I could do anything, I could fight hard until the council arrived.

I wondered in the back of my mind why Johnson thought he could control Danni and glared around. Maybe he had someone up his sleeve that could control Danni and we'd been too distracted to notice. I suddenly had more problems to worry about while I was fighting.

I looked over at Danni who was standing at a distance from everyone, close enough to leap into the fight if she needed. I tried to tell her with my eyes to watch out for an unexpected threat. When she noticed my eyes swaying, in search of the person hidden to us, she understood and looked around.

"Fine by me," Hansel agreed.

All attention was directed my way. There was no way out of this.

"Let's get this over with."

I removed my shirt, exposing my red sports bra and kicked off my boots. The less clothes I had on, the faster my shift when the time came. Hansel stood, wearing only a pair of jeans. He was lean, stretching his broad shoulders out to loosen his muscles.

When I turned to find Danni again, she was gone. I glanced around, searching for her through the growing crowd. A fist plowed into my jaw, disrupting my search.

"Bitch!" I looked up, finding the bouncer from earlier standing over me and moving to punch me again.

I jolted backward, not realizing the crowd had narrowed in, making it harder to evade my attacker. Someone shoved me forward and I ran into the bouncer's fist which pummeled into my stomach. I gasped, air leaving my lungs, and dropped to my knees.

"You should pay attention. First minute has started," Johnson shouted over the crowd.

I hissed out a breath, annoyed by this fight already. I didn't have time to process the pain or the odds stacked against me. My head lifted to find the big brawny guy hunched over and aiming his fist toward my head.

Speedily, I rotated to face him and caught his arm, yanking him downward and twisting, his body flying over me. He slammed onto his back, face squinting from the surprised blow as I mounted on top and rammed my elbow into his face. His arm flew up to fight me off. I swept his arm away and came down with my elbow again. Blow after blow, his flesh opened over the corner of his eye and nose.

His meaty fingers latched around my neck, squeezing tight, and forced my body away. I snarled, using my strength to peel his fingers off, and saw, from the corner of my eye, Hansel mumbling something too low to be heard. He was calling to his magic, and I knew time was against me if I continued to waste it on the asshole beneath me.

I saw my vision swirl, disoriented, when a foot connected with the side of my head. A second werewolf, the man with the ponytail, kicked me as if he were trying to remove my head. The bouncer shoved me off and I flew onto my back as ponytail moved in, leg raised.

My mind snapped into focus, and I spun on the ground, just in time to avoid his booted foot stomping down. My head hurt but I let go of the pain, forcing myself to stand. I burpeed my way up in time to block ponytails leg from slamming into my ribs.

"It hasn't been a minute," I snarled, pointing toward ponytail. I knew it was pointless arguing. This was Johnson's fighting pit, and his rules could change without anyone's approval.

Ponytail moved like a mixed martial arts expert, leaping into a round house kick. I barely escaped, deciding that sparing lives was no longer an option. They were not trying to just get a couple punches in, they were trying to eliminate me permanently. As ponytail landed on his feet, I was on him within a second, fingernails elongated into claws and clamped around his throat.

Ponytail snarled, grabbing my wrist, unable to remove my claws digging into his throat. The bouncer motioned from behind and I turned, yanking ponytail to take my place just as the bouncer hammer fisted ponytail over the top of the head.

Eyes rolled back and ponytail lost balance, his neck snapping. I moved back, bouncer thinking I was trying to catch my breath. I sensed something behind me ready to pounce and moved backward, closer to this werewolf lurking in the crowd, taunting him to come out now. Less than a few feet from the unknown werewolf, I took a breath and stretched my arms out, taunting the bouncer next.

The bouncer's eyes narrowed, flipping me off and then rushed toward me. Just as he was about to reach me the other werewolf leaped into the fight and I spun full circle, jumped behind the new werewolf and reached up, snapping her neck. She dropped to the ground, the bouncer halted, eyes wide with shock. Judging by the rage in his eyes, the werewolf was someone close to him.

"Be thankful I didn't kill her," I hissed. "She will shift and be fine in a few hours. But you...I will rip your throat out if you don't get of my way."

He moved quickly to the werewolf, lifting her into his arms and left through the crowd. I lifted my gaze to Johnson and snarled.

"Bring one more werewolf in this fight, I'll not only kill every single one of them but ruin any chance of you ever running a fighting ring again."

Johnson lifted his arms out. "Just giving the crowd what they want. But message received."

Hansel seemed unaware of me, eyes shut, channeling a magic I couldn't fight head on. Either no one was noticing what he was doing, or they didn't care, and I was at risk of losing. Cautiously, I took a few steps toward Hansel and paused at the power emanating from him.

"How long do you plan to stand there?" I wasn't foolish enough to walk right up to him.

The temperature around him was colder as if his magic had drained his life force. A surreptitious scowl suddenly made me take a step back and I grimaced, not liking where this was going.

"I hope you take no offense when I kill you. It is all to teach her a lesson of obedience." Hansel stalked toward me, positioning for a fight. I did the same, staying in place.

I lifted both hands, tucking my elbows in to protect my body and let myself take a slow breath, calling to my wolf for assistance. My eyes widened, dread and uncertainty overloading my system. I couldn't tap into my wolf because I couldn't find her. My wolf was me and part of me was lost. Trapped under a spell.

I breathed in and out rapidly, alarmed by the realization that I was going to have to fight him without my wolf's assistance. I knew my wolf wasn't gone and only breaking Hansel's spell would bring her back. Clearing my head, I stepped back in time to dodge his punch. His fist sliced through air and I sneered, heaving a kick to his groin.

Hansel blocked it and I moved quickly, slamming my elbow into the side of his head. Hansel stumbled back a few feet and I wasted no time moving in for another attack. He caught my arm as it just reached his head and yanked me forward, twisting me until my back was pressed against his chest.

"I will enjoy crushing your windpipe while my wolf watches," Hansel hissed in my ear.

He squeczed tightly, my vision blurring. I searched the crowd for Danni, not finding her anywhere. I blinked out tears, unable to breathe, reaching blindly for his eyes. Hansel was a few inches taller, so when he leaned back tightening his entrapment, my feet lifted from ground, dangling.

I couldn't channel my wolf's strength to break free. Hansel's magic was crippling in many ways.

"As much as we're enjoying this, it's time to shift." I heard Johnson announce.

Hansel chuckled in my ear. "Good luck with that," he said, and dropped me.

I fell to the ground, gasping and crawled away, trying to recover before he shifted. My ears rang and I shook my head as if that would help, but that only made me wince from the pain engulfing my neck.

"Fuck." I breathed through my nose and reached for my neck as an unexpected round of coughs shook my body. I felt human and I hated it. It was as if Hansel had stripped me bare and given me a new body as a human.

I lifted my head up enough to notice a huge golden-brown wolf standing only a few feet from me. He towered over my frame, making me appear small and fragile. Though I was without my wolf, I was far from weak. I used all my strength to punch him in the snout. My entire body flew into the punch, slicing only through air as he leaped back.

Exhausted, I stood on wobbly legs as if I had 200 pounds of weight on my shoulders, sweat trickling down my back and face. My body had reached its limit and I had barely done anything. It was like every move I made drained me twice as fast. I couldn't understand what was happening and how to break his magical hold over me.

"This how you win fights head on?" I asked.

Hansel couldn't speak but I knew he was listening to every word. His response came with a growl before he moved, too quickly for me to defend myself. His claws raked across my stomach. I bent, grasping my side, and cried out when his canines bit into my shoulder.

I collapsed to my knees and screamed when his teeth bit down harder, splintering my collarbone.

Hansel let go and grunted, his way of laughing. I whirled and watched him walk off to gloat. I dropped flat on my back.

I didn't think I'd lose this easily. Whatever magic Hansel possessed, he was much more powerful than he let on. He got off on people underestimating him. It explained how he was able to control Danni for so long, since she was a potential Alpha. I'd felt her wolf's power and it had not been all of it.

Then a tongue slithered over my face, and I gazed up with blurry eyes, finding a black wolf over me. I tilted my head and saw a woman with her throat ripped out lying next to me. Danni had dragged her body next to me. I bet it was the person who was on Johnson's payroll to assist with snatching Danni when he signaled. She had a familiar sigil tattooed at the corner of her eye. She was a part of a rogue witch organization, and I was sure Johnson had hired her.

I heard shouting in the background. Judging by the commotion, everyone had been enraged and arguing for some time. The ringing in my ears disoriented me and clouded my mind.

Weak and shaky, I lifted my hand, brushing it through her fur as she shifted to her human flesh. Danni now sat over me, moving my head onto her lap as she slid her fingers through my hair.

I winced from my broken collarbone bone.

"I would really like to kill the prick," I grimaced through a ragged breath.

Danni smiled. "I know."

"But his magic..."

Danni nodded. "He's good at pretending to be weak."

Voices got louder in the background, and I was positive they were now outraged at Danni shifting from her black wolf. The secret was out, anger and confusion now directed toward Hansel and Johnson.

"I was trying to tell you with my eyes not to fight him," Danni whispered.

She was ignoring the crowd. Good. That meant we were no longer relevant and that was fine by me.

"Because you knew I would lose?" I asked. Having her beside me soothed my anxiety at being separated from my wolf.

Danni shook her head. "Not necessarily. But..." she lifted her head and stared straight ahead. I'm sure it was

Hansel she was focused on. I was too weak and exhausted to move. "He is more than a werewolf. More than a witch. Those two things combined make him one of the deadliest werewolves out there. He has even fooled me in to believing he couldn't hold up in a fight."

I didn't need to think about it. Hansel was a rarity that not too many lived to tell stories about. Under normal circumstances I would have been more cautious around Hansel, if not for him letting me believe he had weaknesses that were easily exploited.

Hansel's voice was distant but clear enough for me to hear.

"As much as I would like to finish this...I can smell political wolves a mile down the road. But, I would have won if not for the interruption," he argued.

I grimaced, knowing he was right. Not that Danni would have let him kill me.

"But you didn't. It was to the death, if you remember." I found enough strength to glance up and see his smug expression.

"Too bad." Hansel didn't look angry. Then he glanced at Danni and smiled. "The next time I come for you, I'm sure you will be stronger and more resistant to my control. But I look forward to breaking you all over again."

Danni didn't say anything and instead watched him leave. When he was gone, she helped me sit up as I leaned against her.

"His spell will wear off in a few hours, but you should start regaining some strength and healing abilities now."

"Oh, goodie," I complained.

Here I was, stomach shredded, collarbone broken, head spinning from harsh blows and on the verge of vomiting, and neck aching as if someone was trying to squeeze my head off. It could have been worse.

After a minute Danni helped me to my feet, many of the werewolves and humans scattering by the sight of vehicles approaching.

"Are you okay to stand alone?" Danni asked, quickly.

I nodded slowly, still wobbly, trying not to move too fast.

Danni moved quickly and before I could look up and see where she'd gone, she flung Johnson before my feet.

"Nice try," Danni growled. She walked a few feet to her clothes, laying on the hood of a truck near where we stood. She put on her clothes and walked back, smiling. "You have something to say."

Johnson's eyes swerved from me to Danni and then the vehicles pulling into the lot. We couldn't see the vehicles, but we could hear them.

"I swear I'll never enter your uncle's territory again, not that anyone will trust me now." His words were rushed, and I knew he was trying to hurry and avoid the council approaching.

But life wasn't fair. Danni had learned that hard truth. As for Johnson, it was about time he experienced some consequences.

"If I ever smell you anywhere near us, I will hunt and kill you." Danni's tone was unmistakable. If I'd learned anything about my mate, it was that she didn't bluff.

Johnson nodded and tried to scramble away, but Danni slammed her foot down over his leg and I heard a bone snap. Johnson gritted his teeth and shrieked from the pain, not trying to leave again.

"Someone needs to take responsibility for tonight." I lifted my gaze up to three werewolves approaching us. They looked like normal everyday werewolves, except their power was loud enough to deafen.

One of the council agents, I'd recognized once a few years back when I delivered a rogue who had been turning humans without permission. Only an Alpha was allowed to turn a human, and that came with a series of evaluations the human had to endure before the ritual took place. It was the only way to control the werewolf population and keep our secrets from the humans. Furthermore, the changing process could be grueling; not every human survived the transformation.

"Isiah." I wasn't able to take steps yet, afraid I would collapse. I stuck my working arm out instead, offering my hand in greeting.

Isiah looked down at Johnson on the ground, holding his leg and then Danni, standing protectively at my side. An upward crease formed around his lips, brows raised skeptically.

"No offense. But I don't think your new mate approves of me touching you." He smiled in Danni's direction and greeted her with a second nod.

For a council agent, Isiah was one of the youngest. His wolf was over 200 years old but to join the council or to be placed as an agent you had to be at least 300.

His brown eyes swayed back to Johnson, smirking. He easily stood six feet, five inches with a lean build. I'd met him before he became a council agent when I was young, and we dated for about two seconds until I realized I would never like boys. Isiah was a handsome black man with a shaved head and long, dark eye lashes I used to stare at for days. It was his eyelashes and not his masculine features that made me date him in the first place. And of course, his winning personality.

"Take him," Isiah ordered the other two agents standing at a distance. They moved with purpose, picking Johnson up and dragging him to their vehicle. Johnson complained the entire way and I smiled, glad to know he'd no longer be a problem.

"Looks like you went through five rounds," he commented.

I grimaced and instinctively ran my fingers lightly over my neck. The pain was still there but it had dimmed to a subtle ache, barely noticeable unless I touched it.

"That's one way to describe it."

I told him everything that transpired tonight and who Danni was. By the time I was finished, Isiah was taking Danni in for the second time, assessing how much my words held truth.

Isiah was very empathic and was able to see through lies. He wasn't doubting me, only seeing through Danni's eyes if what she'd shared with me was the truth. Then he nodded and I sighed.

"I am deeply sorry for what happened to you," he said. "It is against werewolf law for a child to be turned. Not only can it be painfully overwhelming, but it can be psychologically damaging."

"Have you heard of this werewolf witch, Hansel?" I asked.

If he had and Isiah lied, I wouldn't be able to tell by his impassive expression. The council kept a lot of secrets from packs for reasons I never understood, and I knew Isiah couldn't share everything.

But he surprised me by answering, "Unfortunately, yes." There was a grimace in his tone. "We also heard the

Domina Alexandra

rumors of him spelling a wolf to kill for him. We didn't know it was a werewolf he'd taken at a youthful age."

Danni's eyes were steady, but her posture changed. She had done a lot of things in her wolf form she wasn't proud of. She feared Isiah would try to take her next.

I reached out and squeezed her hand. I wouldn't let Isiah take her, even if he was my friend.

"Then you know how powerful he is. She should not be punished for whatever crimes were committed."

Isiah only studied me and Danni together, taking us in. After a moment, he nodded.

"Agreed. But I will have to share this with the council. There will be a follow-up."

I nodded. "Fair enough."

He smiled. "Your uncle has sent in your resignation to his pack."

I nodded. My uncle moved fast. He wanted everyone to know I no longer held position in his pack and was now classified as a rogue.

"My mate," I said. Danni moved closer. I was still getting use to saying that aloud and believing it. But the way my wolf groveled in Danni's presence, there was no doubt she was my mate. "She is a potential Alpha. And perhaps already more dominant than my uncle. I'm sure now that Hansel no longer has a leash wrapped around her throat, all her power will only make her more of a threat. Besides, you know how much my uncle adores me."

Isiah laughed. One of his agents called out and he sighed.

"Back to my duties." He offered his hand again and I shook it. "Be safe. Both of you. You don't know what it's like to be a rogue and since you are unfamiliar to our laws and pack, no other Alpha will risk taking you in. Especially since you are a potential Alpha."

Danni nodded her understanding. "Thank you."

He nodded. "Duty calls."

We watched him walk off.

The world around me finally came crashing down. What little strength I had left shattered, and my legs gave out.

I was hungry, exhausted, wolf caged and irritable. I had nothing left to give. Danni held me in her arms and leaned in to brush her forehead against mine.

We were an hour from the house, and I wasn't in any condition to drive my motorcycle, let alone be propped up on one.

"Let's get a hotel for the night."

Danni frowned and looked up at the dark sky. There were distant trees in the direction in which she stared, and she smiled.

"It is beautiful out. I'll find us a spot."

It was obvious who was the domesticated werewolf in this new relationship. I smiled, rolling my eyes, and let her carry me off into the great unknown. Life was going to be remarkably interesting with her and I was looking forward to it.

# Epilogue

*Danni*

We'd slept under the moon until the early morning. Karissa's injuries were healed, and her strength was replenished. When we arrived back at Karissa's home, a few members of her old pack members stood on the porch. No expressions could be read but I could see a glimmer of discomfort caused by my presence. I'd ruined Karissa's life in their eyes.

I recognized Karissa's brother Tanner first, who wouldn't acknowledge me. Beside him stood Monica, the woman I'd met the night prior, and another werewolf I didn't recognize.

Karissa's spine straightened as she walked up to them, showing no regret about her recent choice to leave the pack for me. I still didn't know how to feel about that. She was leaving the only home she ever knew because of me and despite assuring me it was a decision she wanted to make, I knew this change wouldn't be easy.

I lingered at her side but gave enough space for her not to feel like I was hovering. My human mind knew they wouldn't harm her, but my wolf had an issue with the distance. I squeezed my fist tight and swallowed the snarl that nearly escaped.

"Come to make sure I survived?" Karissa's tone was playful, but I could hear the tension underneath. She loved each of them but knew they weren't here to check on her safety.

That hurt even more, seeing the disappointment in Karissa's eyes as her brother stood impassively.

"My Alpha wanted to make sure you remembered the promise you made." Tanner couldn't give his sister an ounce of tenderness in his voice. No smile or pain in seeing her leave.

Karissa stood stoically, not replying right away. Instead, she took in the other two standing there with more sadness in their eyes than her own brother. After letting out a breath, Karissa let out a laugh that didn't reach her eyes.

"I guess, like our uncle, you live the identity you are not meant to be in."

Tanner's eyes heated into an amber glow, his chest poking out as if to bolden his posture.

That was enough to send my wolf to the surface. If he shifted one leg, I'd rip it off. His eyes briefly leered in my direction before focusing back onto Karissa in anguish.

I stood proudly as Karissa continued to speak.

"He's no true Alpha and you've always known that, just as much as you were never a Beta. After all, Betas can one day become Alphas on rare occasions and that's what you seek. To steal and lie your way into status like he did."

Through gritted teeth, Tanner snarled. "You don't know what you're talking about." Every inch of his body was stiff as if struggling to decide whether to run or attack.

I stood ready for a fight.

His anger only made Karissa speak more loudly, addressing to the two uneasy companions behind him.

"If he was truly a Beta," Karissa half-heartedly waved her hand toward her brother, "He would never follow my uncle so blindly, without ever questioning him.

It is a Beta's job to question an Alpha's intentions as much as it is my job. She turned her attention back to Tanner. "I hope one day you will accept who you really are before it's too late."

"And what's that?" Tanner questioned.

"A wolf hunter. A position that is honorable. You do that without even realizing it but the greed for more power makes you think you're something you're not. It clouds you. And for that, you will suffer until you accept what you are." Karissa's chin lifted even higher, and I relaxed knowing even if her own brother attacked, she would be able to protect herself. She was always far more capable than me.

But he didn't attack. He only stood there with a shocked expression, as if she'd seen right through his façade. Maybe this was the first time anyone had called him out.

As if to finally submit, Tanner's eyes dropped to the ground before muttering, "You have four hours left."

I watched him and the others leave and turned to Karissa, who wouldn't allow them to see any pain in her eyes, but I did.

Once they were a safe distance away, Karissa whispered, "I should have said these words to him years ago. Maybe then, I'd have the brother I know is inside him."

Comfort was something I hadn't experienced since losing my mom and for years, I doubted if I'd ever feel it again. But as I looked into Karissa's eyes, all I could think about was holding her until the sadness subsided.

Hand steady, I slid my fingers along her cheek, confident in touching her for the first time. A tear trailed down Karissa's face and I brushed it away with my thumb.

"I promise it will be okay."

Our eyes locked, one corner of Karissa's mouth lifting.

"Look who's give meaningful promises now?" Karissa teased.

I took one last step, closing the distance between us and whispered, "I learned from someone who keeps theirs." I brushed my lips over her cheek where a second tear had fallen. "And I look forward to giving you more."

# About the Author

Domina Alexandra is a native of Southern California and currently lives her life as a nomad, never sure of which state she'll land next. She is an author of stories with strong female protagonists, authentic emotions, and thrilling action scenes that mirror her past career as an EMT and Law Enforcement. Not to mention finding unique places that inspire her fantasy universe. She grew up writing poetry as an outlet, and in 2006 she joined a Live Theater program where she played many roles in a production of plays and musicals. During her four years of acting, she fell in love with writing monologues, screenplays, and storytelling. When Domina's not writing or finding new things to explore, she's soaking her feet in the dirt to ground herself, running wild with her dog, Carson, and rewatching her favorite movies and TV shows.

A Rogue's Redemption

# Other Titles Available From Triplicity Publishing

*New Beginnings* by Graysen Morgen. Captain Tristan Malloy has dedicated her life to the Army and takes her job very seriously. When an unexpected situation arises back home, her world is upended. When the dust settles, she makes a choice that will change her life forever. Courtney Hewitt is a third generation Army helicopter pilot, who's been flying in and out of warzones until she gets sent to South America for a Special Forces Operation. The redeployment is a welcomed change of scenery, and the leader of the special forces team she's assigned to work with is an added bonus Courtney can't wait to cash in on, until the alluring captain abruptly kicks her to the curb, ending their secret, torrid affair. When Courtney follows her home on leave and discovers the reason, she must make a choice of her own. Everyone deserves a chance at a new beginning in this action-packed romance.

*An Omega's Grief* by Domina Alexandra. Bonnie's life is finally slowing down, but on a weekend getaway with her mate Rikki, things quickly turn sour when a human is killed right in front of them. Worse, Bonnie has a stalker with an unimaginable power, and if she doesn't confront this dangerous individual, it might cost her pack and friends their lives. With time against her, Bonnie will have to make her toughest decision yet.

*Crossed Reins* by Graysen Morgen. Barrel racing is Carly Rae Walsh's life, until it's ripped out from under her. With nothing to do and nothing to lose, she uses her years of horse whispering skills and intuition to train a troubled thoroughbred racehorse. Allison McKinley is a world class dressage rider who has stepped back from the spotlight to mourn the sudden death of her mother. The last thing she needs when she decides to start training again for competition, is her father's impulsive desire to own a racehorse, and his bizarre decision to choose a rodeo barrel racer as the trainer. The two women have nothing in common except horses, and even that's a stretch. Can they uncross the reins long enough to see what's happening between them?

*Outside In* by Breanna Hughes. Cali Evans is a survivor. Her life hasn't been easy, but her late father raised her to be smart, tough, and dependent only on herself and her wits. On the eve of her 21st birthday she meets Owen Bray - a beautiful and intriguing young doctor who equally frustrates and captivates Cali. That fateful meeting inspires Cali to make a better life for herself. The next day, hoping to make positive change, Cali hops a bus for the West Coast but never reaches her destination. Instead, she wakes up in an underground bunker with no recollection of how she got there. Upon her arrival, she learns that she's one of just forty survivors of a fast-spreading environmental toxin and that human life outside of the bunker has ceased to exist. Tired of the vague explanations and half-answers coming from the people in charge, Cali takes it upon herself to investigate the real reason why she's there and begins to uncover the sinister truth.

*I Love You, Nora Whispered* by Kathy L. Salt. Love in the time of horses and polio. England, 1948. Nora Lakes suffers from post Polio Syndrome and very low self-esteem. When her sister Martha manages to get her a job at

Waterhouse Acre Stables, she can hardly believe it. She had never imagined that anyone would have employed her, damaged as she is. She also never imagined she would meet anybody like Katherine. Katherine Waterhouse was born with a silver spoon in her mouth. She has a mean streak and doesn't like people in general. What she does like, is horses. She wants to be a professional rider but growing up in a conservative house where her choices are limited by her sex, Katherine has always been trapped in her role as a woman. Nora and Katherine - two women with very different backgrounds, drawn to each other with an intensity neither of them is prepared for. Do they stand a chance?

*Omega Rising* by Domina Alexandra. A few months of peace. That was all Bonnie Collins was granted. New trouble has surfaced and go figure, this trouble came with a new pair of claws. When an unknown pack comes to town, Bonnie is forced to make tough decisions that will influence her packs future. Things only get harder when her mate is taken, leaving Bonnie in charge of a pack who still doesn't trust her. With chaos all around, it will be exactly what Bonnie needs to finally embrace what she has become. An Omega Rising. Book 2 of the *Claimed Series*.

*Loose Ends* by Joan L. Anderson. After her estranged sister is killed when she falls onto the subway tracks in Paris just as a train arrives, Allison goes to Paris to deal with her sister's body and collect her things. But, after talking to the police about the accident and viewing the subway surveillance video, something seems odd about her death. When Allison's hotel room in Paris is broken into with only a few things taken, but not any money or credit cards, she begins to wonder if it really was an accident that killed her sister, or if it was murder. Once Allison returns to Washington, D.C. to handle her sister's affairs, she soon realizes that her sister had been living a secret life and wasn't the person she had always thought she was. As troubling things begin to happen to Allison in D.C., she starts wondering if she will be the next person to die.

***Real Love*** by Graysen Morgen. Leigh Myer is a trauma nurse practitioner who is not happy going through the motions of her daily life. When a friend offers up her mountain cabin for a relaxing vacation, Leigh packs her bags. She's never been to the mountains and certainly never in heavy snow. A chance meeting with a fish and wildlife officer turns her idea of a quiet, relaxing vacation…upside down. Camden Gorely loves her job and loves the mountain she works and lives on even more. She's tired of having flings with vacationers who visit for days or weeks at a time, until she meets the elusive nurse from the city. Can Leigh stop running from her past and allow real love into her heart?

***Enticed by Love*** by Lynn Lawler. Henrietta Bailey is a mysterious woman who has spent her entire life living in the town of Crescent, a sleepy beach community in central coastal California. She loves the beach, the ocean air, and the town itself. Her simple life fulfills her. However, she spends much of her time reminiscing about her long-lost love, a woman who left her devastated. Now, another woman awaits on the horizon; a wise, intelligent, and sexy lady who is sophisticated beyond her years. This woman yearns for her soul mate and lover. Will she be able to win Henrietta's heart, or will Henrietta be fated to live the rest of her days alone?

*Love Undercover* by Domina Alexandra. Remi Stone never expected to get the opportunity to work undercover for narcotics. But, when the chance arrives, she takes it. With drugs coursing through a high school, Remi has only until the end of the school year to find the suspects responsible. Undercover, Remi plays her role, moving one step further into the drug industry. She never thought she'd be moving one step closer to the woman who would change her life and take hold of her heart. There is just one issue. Remi Stone is undercover as an eighteen-year-old high school senior. And the woman she can't seem to ignore is her History teacher. There will be a lot of challenges along the way, including one that could cost Remi her life and her heart.

*Playing the Game* by Graysen Morgen. Randi Rojas is a professional soccer player who seemingly has it all, a successful career, a long-term girlfriend, a loving family, and a great group of friends...until a chance meeting with an attractive woman sends her way offside, and into a whole new game. Berkley Ward lives her life to the extreme, spending her days either in the gym or four-wheeling in the woods, and her nights patrolling the streets as an officer. Affairs with taken women are easy, but after years of playing games, she's finished...until she meets a beautiful woman and a game she can't resist. Both women play a dangerously seductive game of cat and mouse, teetering on the edge of friendship and affair.

***Rebel Sweetheart*** by Sydney Canyon. When a headstrong, country music superstar starts getting threatening letters while on tour, her manager has no other choice but to hire someone to investigate the threats and keep her safe. Haley Nielsen is as stubborn as it gets. She does things her way, and her way only. The last thing she needs or wants is a babysitter following her every move and controlling everything she does. Shane Crowley isn't your typical private investigator, or bodyguard, for that matter. She's a former U.S. Deputy Marshal with a lot of experience, and an all or nothing attitude. Tempers flare and the energy burns red hot between the two women as they spend weeks together cooped up on Haley's tour bus, traveling the country. Will they stop resisting each other long enough to see eye to eye? Or will the letter writer make good on his threats?

***A Tale of Spiders and Canned Soup*** by Kathy L. Salt. Living on your own can be hard, but even more so when you're dealing with haphephobia; the death of a twin sister; and a crush on your teacher. Mika is still in contact with her foster family who homes the loves of her life, three young children she would do anything for, when she begins attending University of Aberdeen and meets Pauline, an Australian that teaches Viking history. Neither woman is used to breaking the rules, and their way to each other is a hard one, especially when Mika vows to get custody of the children, whether she is ready to be a parent or not. *A story about growing up. A story about dealing with grief. A story about Mika and Pauline.*

***A Night Claimed*** by Domina Alexandra. Bonnie Collins had plans. And being a werewolf wasn't one of them. Attacked by a rogue who was out to claim her and facing what she now has no choice of becoming, Bonnie can't let go of her human life as a Paramedic. The last thing Bonnie needs is more challenges. However, Rikki, the Alpha of Mill City will be just that. Finding her to be possessive and ruling, Bonnie begins challenging the Alpha's every breath. Finding out her attack was no accident only makes her more angry at the situation. A group of rogues are out to get her. With no clue why, Bonnie has no choice but to seek help from the alluring Alpha and her pack, accepting the new world she was forced into.

*Stunted* by Breanna Hughes. Professional stuntwoman Jessie Knight takes her job very seriously and although she works in the entertainment industry, she has zero desire for fame or notoriety. She also has a very strict no-dating policy when it comes to coworkers. That is, until she meets famous actress Elliot Chase on the set of her new film. The adrenaline rush of the stunts is nothing compared to the sparks that fly between them. After a passionate night together, a sex tape is leaked that sends Jessie and Elliot's private and professional lives into a spiral. Will the fallout be too much for them to last? Or will they find a way out of the mess together?

*Mission Compromised* by Graysen Morgen. Natalia Moreno is thrilled when she arrives in Fiji for a relaxing vacation. However, she soon discovers the overwater bungalow she's staying in has been double booked for the entire stay, and the resort is full. Annoyed and frustrated, she has no other choice but to share her hut with a stranger. Christian Garnier is sent to Fiji for what she refers to as a working vacation, until she finds out she has an ornery roommate for the next two weeks who is dead set on making her job twice as hard. Soon, all hell breaks loose, and the two women are sent around the world on a wild goose chase.

**Stargazing** by Kathy L. Salt. Lissa stared open-mouthed at the GIF that played over and over on the screen in front of her. Heat flushed to her face, igniting her skin. Her heart started pounding in her chest. *Stupid internet, it should really come with a warning label.* She's never been interested in relationships or sex and as the years have gone by she has retreated more and more into her work. Everything changes when she meets Star, a porn actress with a heart of gold and a troubled childhood. *They say that opposites attract, but how much of that is true? What chance do they have when one of them is a virgin and the other one star in pornography?*

**I Belong with Her** by Domina Alexandra. Tajel Pierce loves the thrill of being a paramedic. Every call she goes on gives her a rush. She makes no time for a personal life. No one can ruin her love for her career. Then there is Arianna Castaldi, who just transferred to her new paramedic position in a whole new state. All she needs is a new start without any distractions. Arianna and Tajel's relationship doesn't start off perfect. Embarrassed of the one-night stand Arianna believes she had with Tajel, she wants to pretend they never met and make their relationship strictly business. The only choice they have to keep from strangling each other is to go from denying their feelings to accepting them as they work through intense 911 calls.

***Awakened by Fate*** by Lynn Lawler. Jackie is a woman living life according to her own rules. She's married, but it's the unspoken, open kind. She can have as many female lovers as she likes; she just can't talk about them. After a bizarre encounter turns her world upside down, things slowly begin to change. She finds herself in desperation as she searches for answers. What she discovers is nothing is delivered in a neatly wrapped box. Now that everything has been brought out into the open, she finds she can't run away from her truth anymore. With her new life, comes new responsibilities and a different outcome than what she was expecting. Jackie isn't alone in the story. She meets several new people who help her along her journey.

***Nautical Delights*** by S. L. Gape. Lady Elizabeth Barrington has spent her entire life trying to please her family; constantly opting for a quiet life, she utilises her profession as a doctor to keep out of her families' clutches; bar the annual two-week Caribbean private cruise, where there is simply no budge. Confined to two weeks on board the Iconica super yacht, she intends on keeping her head down and enjoying as much of the holiday as she can, whilst keeping her family at arm's length. Until a crew member catches her eye.

***Worlds Apart*** by S.L. Gape. Hollywood A-lister Heidi Spencer-Brady is everything you'd expect of an Idol. Loved by all, the British Beauty is graceful, talented, humble and so far removed from the 'typical' LA scene. When her husband's infidelity with his new 'leading lady' is leaked, Dawn, Heidi's best friend and manager, goes all out to protect her. She arranges for Heidi to go back to the UK and stay on her cousins farm they had visited as children, much to the disappointment of the animal fearing Heidi.

***Castor Valley (Law & Order Series Book 2)*** by Graysen Morgen. Jessie Henry is torn when she reads about the capture of the Doyle brothers, two young men who were part of her old gang. Unable to let them hang for a crime she's sure they didn't commit, Jessie leaves her wife and the Town of Boone Creek behind and sets out on a journey back to the one place she thought she'd never see again, *Castor Valley*. Ellie Henry watches the love of her life leave, not knowing if she will ever return. When she gets an odd telegram, nearly a week later, she fears Jessie is in trouble. With no other choice, she goes to the one person who can help her.

***Fight to the Top*** by S. L. Gape. Georgia is a forty-year-old, single, Area Director from Manchester, UK who is all work and definitely no play. Having no time to socialise or spend time with her family she prides herself on being fit and well-polished. Erika is an Area Director for the same company, but in the United States. Whilst she is concentrating so heavily on the promotion she has been fighting for, she's starting to feel like her life outside of work is falling apart. The two women are exceptionally different, and worlds apart. Both of their lives are turned upside down when their jobs are snatched from under their noses, and they are suddenly faced with being thrown together by their bosses for one last major project...in Texas.

***Boone Creek (Law & Order Series book 1)*** by Graysen Morgen. Jessie Henry is looking for a new life.

She's unknown in the town of Boone Creek when she arrives and wants to keep it that way. When she's offered the job of Town Marshal, she takes it, believing that protecting others and upholding the law is the penance for her past. Ellie Fray is a widowed, shopkeeper. She generally keeps to herself, but the mysterious new Town Marshal both intrigues and infuriates her. She believes the last thing the town needs is someone stirring up trouble with the outlaws who have taken over.

*Witness* by Joan L. Anderson. Becca and Kate have lived together for eight years and have always spent their vacation in a tropical paradise, lying on a beach. This year, Becca wanted to try something different: a seven day, 65-mile hike in the beautiful Cascade Mountains of Washington state. Their peaceful vacation turns to horror when they stumble upon a brutal murder taking place in the back country.

*Too Soon* by S.L. Gape. Brooke is a twenty-nine-year-old detective from Oxford, who has her life pretty much planned out until her boss and partner of nine years, Maria, tells her their relationship is over. When Brooke finds out the truth, that Maria cheated on her with their best friend Paula, she decides to get her life back on track by getting away for six weeks in Anglesey, North Wales. Chloe, a thirty-three-year-old artist and art director, owns a log cabin on Anglesey where she spends each weekend painting and surfing. After returning from a surf, she stumbles upon the somewhat uptight and enigmatic Brooke.

*Never Quit (Never Series book 2)* by Graysen Morgen. Two years after stepping away from the action as a

Coast Guard Rescue Swimmer to become an instructor, Finley finds herself in charge of the most difficult class of cadets she's ever faced, while also juggling the taxing demands of having a home life with her partner Nicole, and their fifteen-year-old daughter. Jordy Ross gave up everything, dropping out of college, and leaving her family behind, to join the Coast Guard and become a rescue swimmer cadet. The extreme training tests her fitness level, pushing her mentally and physically further than she's ever been in her life, but it's the aggressive competition between her and another female cadet that proves to be the most challenging.

*Never Let Go (Never Series book 1)* by Graysen Morgen. For Coast Guard Rescue Swimmer, Finley Morris, life is good. She loves her job, is well respected by her peers, and has been given an opportunity to take her career to the next level. The only thing missing is the love of her life, who walked out, taking their daughter with her, seven years earlier. When Finley gets a call from her ex, saying their teenage daughter is coming to spend the summer with her, she's floored. While spending more time with her daughter, whom she doesn't get to see often, and learning to be a full-time parent, Finley quickly realizes she has not, and will never, let go of what is important.

*Pursuit* by Joan L. Anderson. Claire is a workaholic attorney who flies to Paris to lick her wounds after being dumped by her girlfriend of seventeen years. On the plane she chats with the young woman sitting next to her, and when they land the woman is inexplicably detained in Customs. Claire is surprised when she later runs into the woman in the city. They agree to meet for breakfast the next morning, but when the woman doesn't show up Claire goes to her hotel and makes a horrifying discovery. She soon finds herself ensnared in a web of intrigue and international terrorism, becoming the target of a high stakes game of cat and mouse through the streets of Paris.

*Wrecked* by Sydney Canyon. To most people, the *Duchess* is a myth formed by old pirate's tales, but to Reid Cavanaugh, a Caribbean island bum and one of the best divers and treasure hunters in the world, it's a real, seventeenth century pirate ship—the holy grail of underwater treasure hunting. Reid uses the same cunning tactics she always has before setting out to find the lost ship. However, she is forced to bring her business partner's daughter along as collateral this time because he doesn't trust her. Neither woman is thrilled but being cooped up on a small dive boat for days forces them to get know each other quickly.

*Arson* by Austen Thorne. Madison Drake is a detective for the Stetson Beach Police Department. The last thing she wants to do is show a new detective the ropes, especially when a fire investigation becomes arson to cover up a murder. Madison butts heads with Tara, her trainee, deals with sarcasm from Nic, her ex-girlfriend who is a patrol officer, and finds calm in the chaos of police work with Jamie, her best friend who is the county medical examiner. Arson is the first of many in a series of novella episodes surrounding the fictional Stetson Beach Police Department and Detective Madison Drake.

*Mommies (Bridal Series book 3)* **by Graysen Morgen.** Britton and her wife Daphne have been married for a year and a half and are happy with their life, until Britton's mother hounds her to find out why her sister Bridget hasn't decided to have children yet. This prompts Daphne to bring up the big subject of having kids of their own with Britton. Britton hadn't really thought much about having kids, but her love for Daphne makes her see life and their future together in a whole new way when they decide to become mommies.

***Rapture & Rogue*** by Sydney Canyon. Taren Rauley is happy and in a good relationship, until the one person she thought she'd never see again comes back into her life. She struggles to keep the past from colliding with the present as old feelings she thought were dead and gone, begin to haunt her. In college, Gianna Revisi was a mastermind, ring-leading, crime boss. Now, she has a great life and spends her time running Rapture and Rogue, the two establishments she built from the ground up. The last person she ever expects to see walk into one of them, is the girl who walked out on her, breaking her heart five years ago.

***Second Chance*** by Sydney Canyon. After an attack on her convoy, Marine Corps Staff Sergeant, Darien Hollister, must learn to live without her sight. When an experimental procedure allows her to see again, Darien is torn, knowing someone had to die in order for this to happen. She embarks on a journey to personally thank the donor's family but is too stunned to tell them the truth. Mixed emotions stir inside of her as she slowly gets to the know the people that feel like so much more than strangers to her. When the truth finally comes out, Darien walks away, taking the second chance that she's been given to go back to the only life she's ever known, but she's not the only one with a second chance at life.

*Meant to Be* by Graysen Morgen. Brandt is about to walk down the aisle with her girlfriend, when an unexpected chain of events turns her world upside down, causing her to question the last three years of her life. A chance encounter sparks a mix of rage and excitement that she has never felt before. Summer is living life and following her dreams, all the while, harboring a huge secret that could ruin her career. She believes that some things are better kept in the dark, until she has her third run-in with a woman she had hoped to never see again, and gives into temptation. Brandt and Summer start believing everything happens for a reason as they learn the true meaning of meant to be.

*Coming Home* by Graysen Morgen. After tragedy derails TJ Abernathy's life, she packs up her three-year-old son and heads back to Pennsylvania to live with her grandmother on the family farm. TJ picks back up where she left off eight years earlier, tending to the fruit and nut tree orchard, while learning her grandmother's secret trade. Soon, TJ's high school sweetheart and the same girl who broke her heart, comes back into her life, threatening to steal it away once again. As the weeks turn into months and tragedy strikes again, TJ realizes coming home was the best thing she could've ever done.

*Special Assignment* by Austen Thorne. Secret Service Agent Parker Meeks has her hands full when she gets her new assignment, protecting a Congressman's teenage daughter, who has had threats made on her life and been whisked away to a Christian boarding school under an alias to finish out her senior year. Parker is fine with the assignment, until she finds out she has to go undercover as a Canon Priest. The last thing Parker expects to find is a beautiful, art history teacher, who is intrigued by her in more ways than one.

*Miracle at Christmas* by Sydney Canyon. A Modern Twist on the Classic Scrooge Story. Dylan is a power-hungry lawyer who pushed away everything good in her life to become the best defense attorney in the, often winning the worst cases and keeping anyone with enough money out of jail. She's visited on Christmas Eve by her deceased law partner, who threatens her with a life in hell like his own, if she doesn't change her path. During the course of the night, she is taken on a journey through her past, present, and future with three very different spirits.

*Bella Vita* by Sydney Canyon. Brady is the First Officer of the crew on the Bella Vita, a luxury charter yacht in the Caribbean. She enjoys the laidback island lifestyle, and is accustomed to high profile guests, but when a U.S. Senator charters the yacht as a gift to his beautiful twin daughters who have just graduated from college and a few of their friends, she literally has her hands full.

*Brides (Bridal Series book 2)* by Graysen Morgen. Britton Prescott is dating the love of her life, Daphne Attwood, after a few tumultuous events that happened to unravel at her sister's wedding reception, seven months earlier. She's happy with the way things are, but immense pressure from her family and friends to take the next step, nearly sends her back to the single life. The idea of a long engagement and simple wedding are thrown out the window, as both families take over, rushing Britton and Daphne to the altar in a matter of weeks.

*Cypress Lake* by Graysen Morgen. The small town of Cypress Lake is rocked when one murder after another happens. Dani Ricketts, the Chief Deputy for the Cypress Lake Sheriff's Office, realizes the murders are linked. She's surprised when the girl that broke her heart in high school has not only returned home, but she's also Dani's only suspect. Kristen Malone has come back to Cypress Lake to put the past behind her so that she can move on with her life. Seeing Dani Ricketts again throws her off-guard, nearly derailing her plans to finally rid herself and her family of Cypress Lake.

*Crashing Waves* by Graysen Morgen. After a tragic accident, Pro Surfer, Rory Eden, spends her days hiding in the surf and snowboard manufacturing company that she built from the ground up, while living her life as a shell of the person that she once was. Rory's world is turned upside down when a young surfer pursues her, asking for the one thing she can't do. Adler Troy and Dr. Cason Macauley from Graysen Morgen's bestselling novel: *Falling Snow*, make an appearance in this romantic adventure about life, love, and letting go.

***Bridesmaid of Honor (Bridal Series book 1)*** by Graysen Morgen. Britton Prescott's best friend is getting married and she's the maid of honor. As if that isn't enough to deal with, Britton's sister announces she's getting married in the same month and her maid of honor is her best friend Daphne, the same woman who has tormented

Britton for years. Britton has to suck it up and play nice, instead of scratching her eyes out, because she and Daphne are in both weddings. Everyone is counting on them to behave like adults.

***Falling Snow*** by Graysen Morgen. Dr. Cason Macauley, a high-speed trauma surgeon from Denver meets Adler Troy, a professional snowboarder, and sparks fly. The last thing Cason wants is a relationship and Adler doesn't realize what's right in front of her until it's gone, but will it be too late?

***Fate vs. Destiny*** by Graysen Morgen. Logan Greer devotes her life to investigating plane crashes for the National Transportation Safety Board. Brooke McCabe is an investigator with the Federal Aviation Association who literally flies by the seat of her pants. When Logan gets tangled in head games with both women will she choose fate or destiny?

***Just Me*** by Graysen Morgen. Wild child Ian Wiley has to grow up and take the reins of the hundred-year-old family business when tragedy strikes. Cassidy Harland is a little surprised that she came within an inch of picking up a gorgeous stranger in a bar and is shocked to find out that stranger is the new head of her company.

***Love Loss Revenge*** by Graysen Morgen. Rian Casey is an FBI Agent working the biggest case of her career and madly in love with her girlfriend. Her world is turned upside when tragedy strikes. Heartbroken, she tries to rebuild her life. When she discovers the truth behind what really happened that awful night, she decides justice isn't good enough, and vows revenge on everyone involved.

*Natural Instinct* by Graysen Morgen. Chandler Scott is a Marine Biologist who keeps her private life private. Corey Joslen is intrigued by Chandler from the moment she meets her. Chandler is forced to finally open her life up to Corey. It backfires in Corey's face and sends her running. Will either woman learn to trust her natural instinct?

*Secluded Heart* by Graysen Morgen. Chase Leery is an overworked cardiac surgeon with a group of best friends that have an opinion and a reason for everything. When she meets a new artist named Remy Sheridan at her best friend's art gallery she is captivated by the reclusive woman. When Chase finds out why Remy is so sheltered will she put her career on the line to help her or is it too difficult to love someone with a secluded heart?

*In Love, at War* by Graysen Morgen. Charley Hayes is in the Army Air Force and stationed at Ford Island in Pearl Harbor. She is the commanding officer of her own female-only service squadron and doing the one thing she loves most, repairing airplanes. Life is good for Charley, until the day she finds herself falling in love while fighting for her life as her country is thrown haphazardly into World War II. Can she survive being in love and at war?

*Fast Pitch* by Graysen Morgen. Graham Cahill is a senior in college and the catcher and captain of the softball team. Despite being an all-star pitcher, Bailey Michaels is young and arrogant. Graham and Bailey are forced to get to know each other off the field in order to learn to work together on the field. Will the extra time pay off or will it drive a nail through the team?

**Submerged** by Graysen Morgen. Assistant District Attorney Layne Carmichael had no idea that the sexy woman she took home from a local bar for a one-night stand would turn out to be someone she would be prosecuting months later. Scooter is a Naval Officer on a submarine who changes women like she changes uniforms. When she is accused of a heinous crime, she is shocked to see her latest conquest sitting across from her as the prosecuting attorney.

**Vow of Solitude** by Austen Thorne. Detective Jordan Denali is in a fight for her life against the ghosts from her past and a Serial Killer taunting her with his every move. She lives a life of solitude and plans to keep it that way. When Callie Marceau, a curious Medical Examiner, decides she wants in on the biggest case of her career, as well as Jordan's life, Jordan is powerless to stop her.

**Igniting Temptation** by Sydney Canyon. Mackenzie Trotter is the Head of Pediatrics at the local hospital. Her life takes a rather unexpected turn when she meets a flirtatious, beautiful fire fighter. Both women soon discover it doesn't take much to ignite temptation.

**One Night** by Sydney Canyon. While on a business trip, Caylen Jarrett spends an amazing night with a beautiful stripper. Months later, she is shocked and confused when that same woman re-enters her life. The fact that this stranger could destroy her career doesn't bother her. C.J. is more terrified of the feelings this woman stirs in her. Could she have fallen in love in one night and not even known it?

*Fine* by Sydney Canyon. Collin Anderson hides behind a façade, pretending everything is fine. Her workaholic wife and best friend are both oblivious as she goes on an emotional journey, battling a potentially hereditary disease that her mother has been diagnosed with. The only person who knows what is really going on, is Collin's doctor. The same doctor, who is an acquaintance that she's always been attracted to, and who has a partner of her own.

*Shadow's Eyes* by Sydney Canyon. Tyler McCain is the owner of a large ranch that breeds and sells different types of horses. She isn't exactly thrilled when a Hollywood movie producer shows up wanting to film his latest movie on her property. Reegan Delsol is an up-and-coming actress who has everything going for her when she lands the lead role in a new film, but there one small problem that could blow the entire picture.

*Light Reading: A Collection of Novellas* by Sydney Canyon. Four of Sydney Canyon's novellas together in one book, including the bestsellers Shadow's Eyes and One Night.

**Visit us at www.tri-pub.com**

www.ingramcontent.com/pod-product-compliance
Lightning Source LLC
Chambersburg PA
CBHW022059170626
46808CB00002B/509